Flash

Fiction!

Vols.1-3

66 MIXED GENRE
SHORT STORIES

S. V. Gilleran

These are works of fiction. Names, characters, places and incidents are the product of the author's imagination or are used fictitiously. Any resemblance to actual events, locales, or persons, living or dead, is entirely coincidental.

Compilation edition cover photo by Lucien Kolly on Unsplash
Individual books cover photo by Martin Adams on Unsplash

To my family and friends,
with grateful appreciation for your
persevering support over many years.

To Marlow

Love
Sean

CONTENTS

The Stories - Vol.1

The Stories - Vol.2

The Stories - Vol.3

FOREWORD

About flash fiction

What is flash fiction? If you're not familiar with the format, a "flash" is essentially a very short story. Usually less than 2,000 words, sometimes as few as a couple of dozen, like a bookish amuse-bouche. A flash can be written in any genre, which makes it an ideal format for an eclectic anthology.

Who writes flash fiction? Mainstream authors have used the format, many of whom you will have heard of (Kafka, Whitman, Hemingway), but increasingly these days indie authors are adopting it, most of whom will probably be unknown to you. Whoever your favourites are, it is an exciting field to explore.

How to write flash fiction? Some stories are time-limited, written to the clock after viewing prompts, usually online. This is like a literary version of brainstorming, where you see the prompts and write what comes, with very little planning. With little time to build full story arcs, the primary aim is often to plant seeds of thought that can grow, or to ask questions that will invite the reader to answer in their own way, translating the story into their own experience. Others stories are word-limited, with or without prompts, so they can be reviewed and edited without time pressure, and as a result may have more structure and plot.

Why write flash fiction? The reasons for writing flash vary. Some authors use it as a way of practising the art of spontaneous creativity, some to test ideas for longer works, but more often as not it is written as an art form in itself. Whatever the motivation, it is fun and accessible to all, so perhaps you might want to try writing flash fiction too?

About the author

I have been writing for a long time, but am only just beginning to publish my own work, thanks to the ebook revolution, and some spare time in retirement to explore it.

Primarily, I'm a story teller, with a mischievous sense of humour and a subtle sense of the macabre. There are a few other senses which are important to me, a sense of curiosity, a sense of adventure, a sense of justice, and as often as possible, a sense of awe. Over the years, I have tried to maintain a sense of perspective too, but I think that might have affected my sense of direction, which may explain how I've ended up here.

Most importantly, I have been lucky enough to meet and share my life with some fascinating people. Partly because of their influence, and partly because of my own mixed European/British/Irish lineage, I like to combine Saxon earthly practicality with Celtic mystical spirituality, in both my life and in my stories.

About this collection

This is the compilation edition of three individual volumes, each of 22 short stories of mixed genre, which are available in the Kindle Book Store on the Amazon website.

The stories came out of my time writing as a member of a small group of indie authors, from the USA, UK and around the world, who come together online to explore and share creative flash fiction. Inspiration is provided by prompts, sometimes pictures and othertimes words, from which we write whatever is drawn out of our imaginations, in just 90 minutes. Sometimes we stay with one theme, other times we write several shorter stories, as the moods, and the muses, take us.

The stories were written over a period of a little under ten years, beginning in 2009. Some are light-hearted, some tongue-in-cheek, some irreverent; others are a little more serious and most have some adult content. Not all of them are politically correct, but no offense is intended and I hope none is taken.

As suggested above, the aim in these very short stories is to play with thoughts and themes and to raise questions rather than provide answers. So a story may not set the whole scene, but it will hint at it, for you to make of it what you will. I think this is more fun but, to offer guidance where some readers might ask for clarification, notes have been added at the end of the book.

Happy reading!

☆☆☆☆☆☆☆☆☆☆☆☆☆☆☆☆☆☆☆

THE STORIES - VOL.1

☆☆☆☆☆☆☆☆☆☆☆☆☆☆☆☆☆☆☆

1☆1. POSEIDON PROMPTS

Susie Reynaud sat at the top of the table, trying to look calm and authoritative, but only too aware of her knees trembling under the polished oak surface.

She breathed deeply, remembering what her mentor had told her, then, turning her salon-coiffured head to the right, she looked first at Teru. A small but intense man with spiky black hair, he was the brightest supernumerary from Mitisaki Corporation. Without saying a word, she slid a photo of a gargoyle towards him. He received it with a slight nod, in reciprocated silence.

Beside Teru sat Chang Lu from Chinese Aerospace, his dark locks smoothed against his pate with, she thought, a little too much gel. She picked up the photo of wrought ironwork and handed it to him, leaning only a few inches in his direction, obliging him to get up out of his chair to reach it.

The tension in her knees was obvious to her now and she placed her feet firmly on the floor to steady herself. As her professionally made-up face moved around to the far left side of the table, she found Poraig eyeing her eagerly, his obvious enthusiasm almost unsettling her composure. She waited a full minute, watching his expression, before scooting the photograph of a flying pig towards him, so fast that he was caught unawares and grabbed at it clumsily.

Still she said nothing, but her lips tightened and there was the touch of a smile at the corners. With a shiver of excitement down her spine, she moved only her eyes to the seat next to her and closed the lids just a fraction, so that Mike Jason, from Australian Aeronautical Associates, could see that she was unfazed by his presence. She waited again, but too long and Mike reached out to pluck the remaining photo off the desk from under her left hand. Damn, she thought, I'm losing it, and she coughed lightly to cover her surprise.

"You know what you have to do," she affirmed in her most efficient voice, "You all have visual prompts, I will take the only written one, and I will remain here in this room throughout the task. Each of you will take your photographs back to your quarters for the next two hours and let them stretch your minds. Put aside all conventional thoughts and let the pictures speak to you through your intuition, as you have been taught. Then bring them back for a plenary session at," she checked her watch with a stiff emphasis, "11am precisely."

Nobody else spoke, so they pushed their chairs back, stood, nodded briefly at Susie, then left. The last one out of the door was Mike Jason and, as he walked through, he looked over his shoulder and winked.

Susie Reynaud sat rigid, letting the electrical spark of his glance diffuse through her limbs, tingling her fingers and toes as it ran to earth. The door closed softly and her shoulders slumped downwards, pressing on her diaphragm and expelling her breath in a short sigh. Damn that man, she thought, damn, damn, damn that arrogant bastard. Then, after taking off her watch and laying it down on the table in front of her, she picked up the piece of paper with the phrase and read it in her head:

"Maybe a dingo ate your baby."

"Stupid bloody phrase!" she said to herself. "What am I going to make of this? And what's it got to do with the price of eggs anyway?"

Five minutes later, she slapped the paper back down on the wooden surface and slouched over to the coffee machine. She felt a touch of panic. Alan's going to be furious if we don't come up with something. Never mind furious, I'll be excluded and that will be the end of my career.

Susie, or Susan as she was thinking of calling herself now, because it sounded more serious, was the last in this group of five to act as task leader. She had survived so far by being non-confrontational, which had won her a reputation of being somewhat lightweight, so she had to prove herself today.

She was sipping her coffee thoughtfully but coughed and dribbled some down her blouse when the door opened with a rush of energy and Alan Lupus, Head of the Outlander Team, strode in.

"How's it going Susie?" he almost shouted and then didn't wait for a reply.

"Sorry to leave you to last, but the report from Tech-Aer Research suggested that you might need a bit of time to warm up. So I let the lads go first. Thing is, we don't have many women on the list so far and I'm counting on you. What do you think of this Poseidon Prompts Project? Pretty nifty isn't it?"

But again, the grey-haired skin-bronzed Kirk Douglas look-alike gave her no chance to speak.

"Dreamed it up myself years ago when we started looking for water engineers to form the first phalanx of our Outlander Team. After all, there's no point in trying to set up communities out there in space until we've solved the problem of water, is there? Of course, we tried real water engineers first, but they had been classically trained, and I could see immediately that they were going to be hopeless when we put them in environments where knowing Newton's laws is about as much use as a chocolate teapot."

Susie gently rubbed the stain on her chemise, hoping he hadn't noticed. He hadn't, and carried on.

"So I wrote a program, using a Monte Carlo generator, to come up with random prompts that, like Zen koans, force people out of their box. It was the advances made in artificial intelligence that made me think of it. We don't need rules of science and we don't need experts who know it all. What we need is a continual stream of beginners who can learn at rapid speeds and make sense out of nonsense and, ultimately, water out of whatever we find out there."

Susie realised that she had made the stain worse. Lupus was oblivious.

"I even thought of bringing in children, but then I realised that these hyper-intelligent aerospace geeks are just like kids anyway. So you've got the best in the world in your team, Susie, and I'm looking to you to bring it all together. Don't let me down." He slapped her on the back, making her gag and dribble some more, then went as swiftly as he had come, closing the door with a bang.

Susie sat down again, disheartened. She fingered the piece of paper on the table.

"Maybe a dingo ate your baby…"

Baby, she thought, baby…. I wonder what Mike's babies will look like. Steady on girl, she admonished herself, you have to concentrate.

Then she remembered her lateral thinking training, picked up a pencil and started to draw a spider diagram. Lines came out of the circled word "dingo" to a baby in a bubble and to "maybe" and "Ben Elton" and dog shows and to a mouth with large teeth and to Little Red Riding Hood and a woodcutter and a little hut in a forest, with roses round the door and a garden and a bride and groom.

She had never really liked either of her names. She'd been called Susie from birth, a good name for a child, but was it holding her back now? Susan sounded more adult, but it was very formal and even saying it made her feel as if she'd done something wrong. Her surname Reynaud had been the source of much teasing at school, where they called her Foxy. It would be nice to change both her names.

She doodled alongside the diagram, testing signatures like a teenager: Susie Reynaud…. Susan Reynaud.… Susan Jason…. Sue Jason.… yes, that was the one, *Sue Jason!* Oh if only.

She was still musing when the others returned.

Accomplished in their own fields, the four scientists were like fish out of water with these Poseidon Prompts. They had each led a similar task during the week's workshop and had made some breakthroughs in isolation, but every time they came together for the plenary, they had reverted to type and analysed, categorised and even indexed their thoughts into a mush of pseudo-creativity that would have had de Bono shaking his head in despair.

Now here they were again, Teru, Chang Lu, Poraig and Mike, all sitting with their knees tucked under the massive oak conference table, their intense, spiky, enthusiastic faces gelled into looks of expectation as they focused on today's facilitator.

Sue stared back.

1☆2. SHORTENING THE ODDS

His father had always impressed on him the importance of shortening the odds in your own favor.

"It's like Sun Tzu said," he proclaimed with emphasis, pulling his copy of "The Art of War" reverently out of the bookcase. "Fight your battles on your own ground."

That was easier said than done when you were a small town travel agent with no fiercer battles to fight other than with shrewd customers demanding ever tighter discounts. But he had gotten the gist of his father's preaching and was applying it in his own way.

There had been a run on lakeside cabins after somebody had spread a rumor round the local college that skinny-dipping was all the rage. He had already made his month's bonus in June with all the bookings he'd taken. Now four co-eds were in front of him giggling with excitement and American Express confidence. He beamed as he pressed "Confirm" for the third week in July. An hour later four young men tried to secure their places with a large cash deposit, but he apologised sincerely and told them that there was none left for that particular week.

When the time came for his own holiday, he wrote out detailed instructions for his assistant, who would look after the shop while he was away. As he walked out the door with an air of anticipation, he jingled the keys to his cabin, surprisingly one of only two that had been rented that week.

Looking up at the sky, he whispered under his breath, "Bring it on, Sun Tzu."

1☆3. THE GREEN MAN

Paige Etting, née Turner, felt the dead weight of her husband heavy on her back as she pushed upwards with her legs. It was the only way she could lift him. She was aiming to get his jacket collar caught on the hook that protruded from the brick recess between the chimney breast and the outside wall. The long mirror that had hung on the hook only minutes before was now propped up on a chair in front of her, so she could see where to direct her effort. It took several minutes and Paige was exhausted when she finally felt the burden ease, the hook now taking the weight. As she began to lower herself gently downwards and let go of the body, his head flopped to one side and she caught site of his face, beside hers, in the mirror.

"Go on and stare over my shoulder you pig," she said, "in death as in life – forever!"

The last ten thousand words of her novel eased themselves onto the page with no further interruptions or criticism from Ed. Without his voice constantly in her ear, she sometimes awoke from her focus to wonder whether she'd gone deaf. She'd never known such peace and she finished the work in only two weeks. By that time the plaster was dry.

Twenty years ago, when she married Ed, he had heartily approved of her ambition to become a writer. He had seemed so supportive when she lacked confidence.

"You really think I can do this?"

"Of course, my darling, and if you get stuck now and then, I will offer what assistance I can with a few prompts, just here and there."

At first, that had worked and she found his insight to be helpful when she ran into difficulties. But then a few prompts when she was stuck turned into her getting stuck on his prompts. He started to read everything she wrote and there was never a time when he didn't express an opinion, even if it required a major revision of plot and characters. Just when she thought the end of a novel was in sight, Ed would highlight flaws and inconsistencies and that closing chapter fell back again behind the horizon. Would she ever finish anything? Well, she had enjoyed putting the final flourishes on the pargeted Green Man she had moulded onto the fresh plasterwork behind her, the mouth open but silent, spouting laurels instead of pessimism.

Two years ago she had fallen into a depression and this came out in her writing as she moved away from romance towards crime. Her head filled with thoughts of murder and her stories began to explore every which way to kill and dispose of a body. Strangely enough, Ed seemed to relish the development. Not a natural romantic himself, his criticisms until then had been mostly on her use of language and the continuity, but with this new direction he became even more intrigued by Paige's plots and protagonists. He now hovered behind her all the time, not even waiting for a natural pause before pointing out where she was going wrong.

"You can't throw the body down a well," he would say, "it's bound to be discovered."

"No, not poison," he argued, "that was out of date a hundred years ago. These days whatever you buy is going to be traceable. What's wrong with a simple blow to the back of the head?"

"Now you're really being silly, darling," he scoffed, "how could a 100lb woman carry a 200lb man? Unless, that is, she used her legs and back, like a weight lifter."

She glanced back over her shoulder at the face on the wall, a ghastly but now serene reminder of the intelligence that had supplied her with the final plot.

"Thank you Ed," she said to herself, "for such cleverness and such stupidity. I could never have dreamed all this up without your prompts."

Turning back to her desk, she opened the email she had received from Ed's computer a fortnight ago:

"My Darling Paige, I don't know how to say this to your face, so please forgive me for using this impersonal medium. Over the last twenty years I have supported your writing and no-one is more delighted than I to see you achieve success. It would be churlish of me to say that I am envious, but you know as well as I do that my input to your work has been invaluable. Will I always be content to stay in the background, looking over your shoulder? I think not, so I have decided to write my own books. If I stay with you, we will inevitably be drawn into discussions about your work, so, when you open this email, I will have already left to travel far away, to gain the peace and quiet that is needed to write for myself. I am sure you will understand. One day, we may meet again, but until then, I suggest that you make your own plans for the future.

Your loving husband, Ed."

She closed her laptop and got up to make a cup of coffee.

"That email was your best idea," she mused.

1☆4. CUTTING A DASH AND PASTING IT

I'm not one for rushing, but there are times when you have to make a dash for it.

Like the other day, when the mailman was later than usual and I couldn't leave for work until the check arrived, what with my account in disarray and the rent overdue.

Missed the train after that and caught the eye of my boss as I ran through the lobby.

Why is life so complicated sometimes? It's not as if I hadn't done my bit. Staying up into the wee small hours night after night collating and editing and reviewing again and again. It would help if we could use the new software that laid everything out automatically, recognising the difference between m and n dashes, adjusting the leading and the kerning without having to use those stupid metal rulers, but no, this particular publication still worked with cut and paste, and I mean cut and paste. That scalpel's gone through countless layout boards and more fingernails than I care to remember. Then that spray stuff gets everywhere, on fingers, up noses, in eyelashes, and even on the cat's whiskers.

So why is it that, when I most need time to be on my side, the clocks speed up and the calendar leaves drop faster than a maple in the fall?

He wasn't my usual, of course, the mailman I mean. He was

some student fill-in with a smirk and a leer and a ready line in housewives after breakfast, to whom he liked to deliver his package, if you see what I mean, missus. Only he took one look at the state of my spraymounted nightdress and my inky-black eyes and stepped backwards so fast he nearly fell off the porch. Signature required but all he got from me was a squiggle and a tsk.

Then upstairs to shower and change and run a re-mascara'd eye over the mirror and out the door again without so much as a pop tart.

1☆5. PRIVY COUNCILLOR

"For the last time sis, I'm not going to go. This town is where I belong now. As a Councillor I have my responsibilities. I can't take off for three months just because you say he's poorly again."

Linda walked over from where she was brewing coffee and opened the photo album on the table in front of Dylan.

"Look at these," she said, "don't they mean anything to you?"

"Such as?"

"Well, look at mum here, sitting on the running board of the old Ford, laughing. That was when we had that picnic, remember? All five of us..."

Linda stopped and bowed her head. She shouldn't have counted.

Dylan ran his finger over the glossy surface of the photo.

"Can't see that it would make much difference now if I went back."

He turned the pages slowly, then looked up at his sister.

"I can't believe it," he said, "he's only taken a photo of that old outhouse. Why would he do that?"

"I don't know, but none of us will ever forget it, perhaps he felt the same."

"Ha!" Dylan gave a mocking laugh. "I doubt it."

Linda went back to get the coffee.

"He does have feelings, you know."

"Listen, sis, I'd rather spend a month in the town jail than another hour locked up in that privy. It was inhumane…."

"I know, but that's all in the past now."

"No it isn't, that's the point, it's why I'm so passionate about the Orchard Project here, and why I'm going to stay until it's up and running. We shouldn't be locking up kids in this day and age."

Linda laid two hot cups of coffee softly on mats and edged her denimed bottom up onto the table sideways, her knee crooked beside the album. She lifted the cellophane page cover and picked up the photo, holding it up to the light.

"I wonder what happened to that car. I haven't seen it since mum died, and Gary never mentioned it. Do you think I should ask dad?"

"Why not? Might give him something else to think about."

"Why don't you ask him? Cars is a boy thing."

"I've told you sis, I'm not leaving here. You can stay as long as you want, but when you go, I'm not going with you."

"It's a pity, that's all. I mean for your sake, more than his."

"You're wrong, Linda, I'm staying here for my sake. When I get that project set up, I will feel as if all those hours locked in that privy finally mean something."

Dylan ran his fingers through his long hair and moved towards the door.

"I've got be somewhere sis."

"You haven't drunk your coffee."

1☆6. PLANTATION

It had taken me fifty years of focus, dedication, and unbelievably hard work to build. A plantation covering hundreds of acres, every single one of which had been cleared and nurtured, year after year, changing the soil from an infuriating chalk to a rich loam by carrying silt from the rivers in buckets hung from a yoke across my shoulders.

Why I did it was obvious. It was for her. It was my gift, my temptation, my Lyrebird arbour. How could she resist? And yet she did, year after year. Oh, she'd come and stay for a few weeks at a time, and we'd make exquisite love, and she seemed to be happy. But then I could see something in her look, the way she'd move her eyes just a fraction of an inch off my line of sight, and I knew she was going leave again.

She'd never say what was missing that opened a hole in our ecstasy. She left that for me to ponder, and so I'd try to guess. I created a garden for her, with flowers of her most loved colours and scents. When she returned, I sensed the joy in her heart, and she spent hours of every day sitting in the swing seat, reading or musing with a far away gaze. Or she'd walk slowly round the beds, touching the petals with gossamer fingers. But, after only a month, she came into the house, packed and disappeared.

When I say "house" I guess I mean shack. The work on the land took all day and by the evening I was tired and content to sleep on a rough timber platform in an equally shabby cabin. She'd never complained and our lovemaking never suffered from any hint of dissatisfaction. But now I resolved to build her a proper house, with verandas where she could sit in the shade or the cool of the evenings.

On her next visit, the ground floor was completed and she stopped on the path with visible surprise. Then she laughed and ran to hug me. The following year, I'd added another storey with a balcony so she could enjoy the perfumes rising from the garden. The year after that, there was a third storey where we could drink wine, eat the fruits I'd grown and listen to the cicadas before retiring for the night.

That was the best time and I thought our happiness was complete. We were almost as one, until that look returned and my bliss was shattered, changed in an instant into a fear so profound as to make me retch deep inside.

I'm an old man now and she hasn't been here for the last five years. She's still alive and still single, I know, because I read about her now and then. It's been reassuring, knowing that she's never chosen another man to be with. But this morning I saw a photograph of her at the Oscars and, although she looked more beautiful than ever, the camera had captured her face in a way that froze that look, with her eyes just a millimetre off to one side. And then I knew. Even if she came back, she'd leave again and my fifty-year belief, that eventually we'd be together forever, was foolish.

So I ploughed the garden back into the plantation and abandoned the house, which has fallen into neglect. I'm ready to die now, but I'll end my days in the old shack, on the wooden platform.

1☆7. SUN, SEA, SUSAN

It wasn't my first trip to the beach with her, but it was the most memorable. Not for any of the usual reasons, with the sun stroking our skins or the sand stinging our softer parts or the sea slapping at our swimwear as we paddled thigh-deep to brave the initial chill of immersion. No, it was none of these that stayed particularly in my memory, but the silly simple game we played afterwards.

"Write them down," she said, "I brought a pad and pencil."

"Isn't this a bit foolish?" I asked.

"Totally, but so what?"

I had to agree, there was a certain synergy in the mix, saying them out loud then spelling them slowly as I marked them down, one by one.

"Even the obvious ones?"

"Yes of course. Even the three-letter shorties. They all count."

I licked the pencil and began: sun, sea, Susan, Simon (that's me) and sandwiches. I had hoped that they were salami, but she'd made peanut butter and jelly and they were the rules, I had to be able to see, smell, hear or touch them.

"Say them again, speak confidently, then tell me how they

link to something you really want to do."

"Sun - ever since I was ten years old and watched Neil Armstrong make his giant leap for mankind, I'd wanted to be an astronaut. It never happened, of course, but that didn't take away the desire."

"Sea - Jacques Cousteau was my favorite at the time. I used to hold a lolly stick in my mouth and breathe with a noisy hiss as I waggled around on the carpet, burning my knees with abandon. That might even have started it, but it was too long ago for me to remember."

"Susan…"

Now I was entering into the spirit of the game and I'm quite sure she knew what was going through my mind. I spat it out.

"Sex."

That, she said, was breaking the rules. I said I could see it in my mind's eye, but she insisted that if I was going to use a word, it had to be real. So she grabbed hold of me, pushed me down on my back, and flipped the blanket over us.

But that's not the memorable part. What stayed with me after that day playing with the S words was the lasting effect it had on my speech.

She'd cured my lisp.

1☆8. MOTHER DEAR FATHER

Tightening the cord on his blue flannel pyjamas, Philip padded softly into the kitchen to find Freda sitting at the table, her pink towelling robe wrapped around her drooping frame.

"You couldn't sleep either?" he said with a consoling hand on her shoulder.

"No, of course not," she answered with a sigh to end all sighs. Her own hands were clasped loosely on an open copy of Cosmo, the words unread, the photographs unseen.

"You heard them then?" He clocked her slow nod as he pulled out the drawer with his pipe and tobacco. Smoking this early was not his way, but something had to be done to calm his nerves.

She turned to him, her eyes searching for reassurance in his face. "What are we going to do Pip?"

His left eyebrow lifted, only a fraction, but it was enough to convey the strength she had come to rely on over the years. "We will do what we agreed. It's the only way."

A muffled movement upstairs and the closing of the bathroom door told them that at least one of the twins was up.

"It'll be today, then," she breathed, turning back wearily to stare through yesterday's flowers arranged sadly in the vase in the middle of the table. Mothers' Day flowers.

The noises above grew more certain, recognizable now as feet.

"Head's up, Freddy," he cautioned, using her childhood name, "incoming!"

The feet stomped and flapped down the stairs and onto the kitchen tiles, one pair in Doc Martens, the other in flip-flops.

"Good morning Sam, good morning George." Philip stood by the stove, the lines of his jaw at perfect right angles to his square set shoulders. "Happy birthday to both of you."

"Good morning father, good morning mother," in perfect chorus, albeit an octave apart.

"I was just about to cook some breakfast. Eggs over easy?" a frying pan in his right hand, tracing a lazy figure eight in the air.

"Er, thanks, but no thanks, we're off to a meeting. But," and here Sam stopped and stuttered a little as he saw his mother's expression.

"But?" Freda repeated, drawing out the hesitation, underlining the question.

George stepped in front of her brother and pulled out a chair out from under the table. "But, mother, we have something to say first, now that we're of age." She positioned her Levis over the seat and hovered, as if waiting for permission, which came from her father's eyebrow.

Flip! The silence was cracked as Sam took a step forward. His body went rigid as he spoke.

"We are going to town. We're going to see someone. About…" Sam glanced at George, but hardly paused for breath, his words falling over themselves in his self-conscious rush.

"… About a transsexual operation. For both of us."

Flop! Following through his hurried sentence, Sam looked for an escape, a diversion, a release of the tension, and found it in the kettle. "I'll make you some tea, mother, you look as if you've been up all night."

Philip's instinctive sense of protection was around Freda even before his arm was. "We both have, and not just this night, we've known what you were going to say for months now, and we've been worried sick."

George stamped her boots in unison, her own way of dealing with conflict. "Well you shouldn't be, there's nothing to worry about, and anyway, it's not your life. It's mine, and Sam's." Her voice tailed off as something in her mother's face shook her very insides. Something she'd never seen before, so deep and so knowing.

Flip! Now Sam was at his sister's side. "Don't start on about it being unnatural, or saying that we're letting you down, the way you've nurtured us, we know all about that argument. It's in our genes, we can't help it." Then he, too, saw the look in his mother's eyes.

"What?" they begged, both together. That chorus again. Note-perfect split-second timing.

Philip put down the unwanted pan and took command in his most gentle voice. "Sam, George, we have something to tell you. Sam, I suggest you sit down as well." He cleared his throat. "Your mother and I, we, are no strangers to that argument or any other on this point. How can I put this? We agree with you. It *is* in your genes." He paused, not for effect, but because he was genuinely stumped for a way to tell the truth.

Now it was the kettle's turn to split the quiet by steaming and clicking before settling down to listen. Philip fished.

"Michelangelo once said that the angel was already in the marble and that all he did was chisel away until he set him free. Shakespeare said that men and women are merely players on the world's stage, and that each has many parts. We know. We've been there."

"Pip, don't." Freda started to sob, her long hair falling in front of her face.

"Yes Freddy, we must, they're old enough now, and they've brought the subject to us."

"You see," Philip went on, "when we were your age, your mother and I, that is to say, your *father* and I, felt the same way. But we decided to get married and have a child first, just in case anything went wrong later. We were lucky enough to have twins, a boy and a girl. But then we went ahead. It was a very difficult time, but we both felt released when it was over."

Sam and George, open mouthed but speechless, turned from their mother to their father, their father to their mother.

1☆9. CHILDREN'S CORNER

"Avec les tendres excuses pour ce qui va suivre."

"Psssst! Claude! Can you hear me?"

"Murrgggle."

"Claude! I can't move my legs."

"Ngggnnmmmm."

"Goddammit Claude. What's the matter with you? I'm telling you, I can't move my legs. And I think my left arm is broken. What in hell happened?"

"Schhummm kinda banggg."

"I feel like I've been trampled by an elephant."

"Yooooo wurrrrr. Weee bbboth wurrr. It wasss jjjjjiiimmmbbo."

"For goodness sake Claude, stop mumbling, you sound like your mouth is full of cake."

"Mmmmmaaarrr…"

"Come on Claude, stop muttering, spit it out man."

"Mmmmaaarrrschhippppann."

"Well thank goodness that broke your fall, it's softer than this board. What's all this white stuff?"

"Schhno darnnsssinggg, yooo'vve misssed yorrr turrnnn."

"Have I? Can't worry about that now. I'm cold. My legs are icing up. I'm going to try raisin' my head. No, it's no good, you'll have to go for help. Can you walk?"

"Nooo. Caaarrn schtann uppp."

"What do you mean you can't stand up? That's just typical of you Claude. Always so contrapuntal. Now stop being so sheepish and go round up some help. Come on, you'll be on soon."

"Nooo gooood. Caaarrnt waaalllkkk."

"Shhh! Did you hear that? I think the cat's coming. Oh no! Go away! Shoo shoo!"

1☆10. PREMONITION

On the morning of my fifteenth birthday I woke up in a cold sweat, my PJs clinging to my body like glad wrap. I felt sick, a deep sense of unease, as if I was hanging upside down over the john, wanting to wretch. The dream, so vague, yet so vivid, sat on my chest like cough mixture, burned down my throat, hazing my vision.

Cold water on my face didn't help and I zombied down the stairs in my bathrobe.

"Hey Mickey," said mum brightly, "first driving lesson today."

"Oh, yeahhhh…" I said, but then stopped, looking to my left. What was that? A memory? A faint recollection came into my head. Driving. The dream emerged in gray colors and subdued sounds, just enough for me to know that there was something bad about driving.

Mum looked at me with her head on one side. "Well don't sound so goddam pleased about it," she said.

"Sorry," I said automatically.

"Eat your breakfast and get dressed," she said, "I've got to take Joey into town to buy his first pair of shoes. So big day for both my boys."

Dad came into the kitchen and scruffed my hair. "Hurry up son. I can spare half an hour before I have to go to the depot."

"Oh, yeahhhh…" I said without thinking, but then "actually dad, I'm not feeling too good this morning, can we put it off until later?"

Dad put his head on the other side. "What? Oh OK, I'll see if I can get off early."

But when dad returned from work that afternoon, I wasn't feeling any better. By that time I had pieced together some of the vivid parts of the dream and had made my mind up that I wasn't going to learn to drive. Not unless I wanted someone's death on my conscience, because that's what the dream was telling me, that the day I started driving I would kill somebody.

Over the next few days my mum and dad gave me some leeway. They must have thought that I had a bug and I didn't tell them anything different. I didn't tell them anything at all, how could I? But after a week, I could see they were getting pissed with me.

"Don't you think you're being a little selfish Mickey?" mum asked. "I've got my hands full with Joey and feeding the lot of you. I could do with a little help with grocery errands now and then. It would be a lot easier if you could drive."

But drive I didn't. Wouldn't. Couldn't, unless I could shift that dream. Every time I weakened, every time I thought I was being stupid and that I'd have just one lesson, the dream came back and I'd wake up drenched again. This went on for weeks and then months until a year had passed and it was my sixteenth birthday. By that time my friend Jim had his own car, an old Chevy with dented bumpers and a cracked windscreen. We were out on the back roads, swinging wildly from side to side, tiring up the dust behind us like Road Runner taunting Coyote. Jim was singing and I was laughing when he handbraked a full hundred and eighty degrees and scrunched to a stop, the dust now blowing into our faces.

"OK, Mickey, your turn," he said.

"What? You gotta be kidding," I said, wiping my eyes. When I opened them again I could see that he was deadly serious.

"I said it's your turn. If you think I'm going to be doing all the driving when we're out enjoying ourselves, you ain't coming. You have to do your share. It's your *duty* man."

I put my hand on my guts: no rumbles. I stuck two fingers into my neck: my pulse was fine. I stared at the dashboard: my eyes were clear. I felt excited.

"Yeah, alright."

My first mistake was to start off in reverse with the wheel on hard lock. I hit some rocks, but Jim just guffawed. Lurching forwards, I managed to get the front left wheel caught in a rut and lost control again, the steering wheel spinning through my hands. By the time we got to the old silo, Jim was snorting like a mule.

"Hey man, you're downright dangerous!" he said, through gulps of breath.

But I had forgotten the dream, caught up in the thrill, and

pressed the gas pedal to the floor. At sixty miles per hour I couldn't keep the Chevy on the road and we couldn't keep our asses on the seat. I was alive and ecstatic.

When I walked into the kitchen later that afternoon, mum smiled at me and said, "well, did you enjoy it?"

"Goddam right I did…" I said, then "…hang on, how did you know?"

"Jim took Joey out for a drive yesterday, so I could get his room decorated. Then as I was painting I thought to myself how great it would be if you could do that now and again. So I asked him to give you your first lesson. Guessed it might be different with him." She smiled again and pointed to a pile of insurance forms on the table. "I've got to fetch something from the store. Why don't you look after Joey and fill out one of those while I'm gone?"

"No, mum, wait…." But she had already gone out the door.

OK, I thought to myself, I've had my first lesson and nothing has happened. I haven't killed anybody. Perhaps the dream was just a dream. So I picked up a pen and started writing.

Forms! Don't you just hate them? Why is it that you fill out one box and then find you've already answered the question in the next box? What a waste of paper I thought as I screwed up page after page and tossed them over my shoulder. After half an hour, though, I had a completed and presentable offering.

Nodding as I checked through, I chuckled at mum's underhand scheming. But she was right, I would be able to help with the groceries and Joey. Joey? He's very quiet I thought. Then my chest squeezed and my guts loosened and I rushed into the lounge. Joey was lying on the sofa, on his side with his back to me, not moving. On the floor behind him were what looked like chewed up insurance forms.

"Joey!" I shouted and ran to turn him over. His face was blue, his eyes were staring, and a little strip of paper was hanging out of his mouth....

1☆11. SUCH SMALL HANDS

The only woman I have ever loved has such small hands. Exquisitely formed but doll-like, as if, as a child, she'd stolen the fingers of a Jumeau Bébé. But as small as they are, I've never known such power to be passed in a simple touch; a stroke of the wrist, a scratch with a nail, a tickle with a fingertip, a squeeze in a palm, a gentle pummel with a fist.

For seventeen years these tiny hands held my life, my hopes, as I held my breath every 14th of February, pulling from my pocket the smallest of boxes with the smallest of rings. Every year she sighed and gently reached for my own indelicate paws and patted them, very slowly, with more love and sensitivity in her such small hands than I have in my whole body.

1☆12. REMEDIAL CONSEQUENCES

Sally stared at the clear plastic bag of saline and watched the drips fall down the tube into Chloe's arm. She was perplexed. What could have happened? Why was Chloe lying here in a coma? What had gone wrong? Chloe's father would be here within minutes. How was she going to explain this?

It was only a week ago that she had started her new job in the real estate office and had been an instant success. That morning, Monica was displaying obvious signs of distress, refusing to answer the phone, drinking diet cola with abandon, rushing out to the john and returning with red eyes and blotched mascara. As the new girl, Sally didn't feel able to join in the crowd around Monica offering solace and empathy. But at lunchtime she had slipped off home to walk around her garden until the answer came to her.

Back in the office, she placed a small vase on Monica's desk. In it was a delicate orchid with petals shaped like an umbilicus, a rare specimen called Rumi's Navel. Monica stared at it through her tears, breathed in its scent, and gradually her sobbing subsided. She turned to look at Sally and mouthed "thank you." Everyone else then stared at Sally, their eyes wide and questioning.

The next day April sauntered over to sit, casually, on the corner of Sally's desk.

"How did you do that yesterday?" she asked.

"Oh, sometimes there are just things that you know," said Sally, taking a tissue out of a box and dabbing her lips.

April shrugged and walk away, but that afternoon she was back to explore.

"I'm having a little trouble sleeping…."

"Not uncommon."

"Is that one of the things you know about?"

Sally nodded, pursing her lips.

"Let me think about it."

The next morning, Sally was up early as usual, walking round her garden in her dawn ritual. "Yes, that one," she thought to herself and reached down to pluck two leaves.

"They're called Squirrells' Dreams," she said to April later, "stir them into boiling water, wait for it to cool, then drink it before you go to sleep."

Throughout the morning there was a queue of questioners at her desk, asking about boyfriend anxieties, menstrual pains, chocolate addictions, and even split ends. Sally smiled and noted them all down.

The next day she returned with a basket full of flower petals, shoots and leaves. Her popularity was assured and when April arrived at 10am, having slept through the alarm, a Hershey's Bar appeared on Sally's mouse mat.

Mr Jackson, the realtor, seemed oblivious to the change in mood in his staff. This was odd, because he was normally in and out of his room, picking up on this and that mistake, scribbling on letters and documents, highlighting what had to be changed or deleted, and then asking what the hell had gotten into people. Now he just wandered through the office grinning and winking at the girls, who smiled back. Occasionally he would pop his head round the door and say, "Sally, could I have another cup of your delicious coffee?"

He didn't notice when Lizzie had a whole morning of gabbling utter nonsense on the phone to his most important clients. He didn't notice when the temp, Michelle, walked a zig zag path to the kitchen, deliberately stepping on every edge of the carpet tiles.

Life in the office was peaceful, just as Sally liked it, until Mr Jackson's daughter, Chloe, called in for a chat with the girls. After an hour's laughter and mock-charades about her college tutors, Chloe asked Sally out to lunch, as she had something delicate to discuss.

The saline drips were mesmerising. Sally awoke out of a dreamlike state and knew exactly what to do. She reached into her bag and pulled out a tincture bottle and a syringe. With the steady hands of someone who believed in herself, she loaded the syringe and pieced the saline bag, squeezing the plunger.

As she walked down the hospital corridor past the nurses' station, Sally caught sight of the red lights flashing and heard the professional response to an alarm.

"Crash Team, Room 42!"

1☆13. LUST IN TRANSLATION

She was sixteen, slightly deaf and semi-literate, perfectly suited for monotonous shifts in the bakery. He was sixty, straight-backed and shameless in his insistence on Lederhosen and stentorian pronunciation.

She opened up the door to the back alley and he entered for their early morning ritual, a lingual slap and tickle that was foreplay for the boring day ahead.

"Guten Morgen meines Mädchen." [*Good morning miss.*]

"Good morning sir, what would you like today?"

"Kaffee bitte." [*Coffee please.*]

"Cup of coffee coming up, but you won't want it bitter. How about some sugar?"

"Ja, ein Kissen." [*Yes, a sachet.*]

"No kisses for you, you old goat. What about a sausage roll?"

"Wurst?" [*Sausage?*]

"What a cheek, they're our best."

"Vielleicht eine Torte?" [*Perhaps a tart?*]

"You feel like a tart?"

"Ja, Obst mit Schlag." *[Yes, fruit with whipped cream.]*

"What did you call me? An obstinate slag???"

The old man stiffened and tapped on the counter glass with a rigid finger, pointing to the left of her cherry buns.

"Oh, you mean the tart, fruit with whipped cream?"

"Ja." *[Yes.]*

"Just the one?"

"Nein." *[No.]*

"Nine? That's a lot of tarts for a skinny old man."

"Fünf." *[Five.]*

"Gesundheit!"

His left hand moved up over the top of her display and with the other he touched each finger tip in succession.

"Ein für mich *[one for me]*, Ein für meine Frau *[one for my wife]*, Ein für Kurt *[one for Kurt]*, Ein für Willi *[one for Willi]*, und Ein für Hans *[and one for Hans]*.

Ich kaufe viele *[I buy many]*."

"Cop a feel? You'll keep your hands to yourself!"

"Und Ein für Sie." *[And one for you.]*

"Oh, now you're fussy? So what's it to be then?"

"Sechs." *[Six.]*

"Right, that's enough of that, off you go."

She tossed a handful of creamy cakes into a bag, thrust it in his open palms and gave him a light smack on his leather cheeks as she bundled him back out into the lane. Before she closed the door she shouted after him.

"Hey, Fritz, same time tomorrow?"

"Ja." *[Yes.]*

"Bring Willi next time."

1☆14. HERORIST

I've never worked for a living and have no intention of starting now.

What's different that should compel me to review my approach to life? Just about everything I can put my lazy articulate mind to. Don't get me wrong, it's not apathy, as I am acutely interested in me and mine and every living organism that surrounds and affects my comfort.

At school I was a complete bastard but, as the rest of my dorm matched my level of detached and amused sadism, I didn't really stand out. You might even say that I fitted in… hmmm… what's the best word here… snugly?

Then after three years in the Service, during which time I didn't even get my tailored cap wet, I came out with an invitation to join the Drones Club and from there it was, well, plain sailing. Until, that is, the warped winds of revolution wafted up the carpeted stairs to swirl around the leather chesterfields and disturb my peace.

Oh, a challenge? The lumpen have no idea how to follow through what they myopically believe that they have started. They don't have the brains or the guts, and they have too much heart, driving forwards for sincerity, equality, freedom, fraternity and the rights they hold so dear (the right to live and breathe and fornicate and drink gallons of beer). They're prepared to work for it too, the fools.

For myself, I like to surf on the tide of rebellion and let the sea of change take me with it. Say the right words in the right tone of voice at the right time in the right place and, all of a sudden, you're a hero. Up with the periscope and scan the horizon and you soon see who's who and where the power lies. A quick-fingered trigger and a shot in the right direction, below the surface of course, and someone falls over. A vacuum, a gap in the hierarchy, ready-made and yet bespoke with my measurements.

That's the irony of leadership in any insurrection, officers use ratings to remove other officers, just like changing the rota, only it's permanent, at least for a few years. So I was happy to join in and do my share and support the killing, the bombing, the sniping, the multi-level planning of genocide, as long as I was on the winning side.

When the first wave fell and I was caught, nothing really changed because I was still an officer and prison was no worse than the Club. A bath a day for twelve years did nothing to dampen my spirit. The ratings who brought my food were no different to those who had polished my shoes before. And I knew that this, too, would pass.

The second wave was as inevitable as daylight. Now I'm a hero again, feted for my courage and steadfast resolution in the face of decadence and privilege upheld by, well, those poor bastards with whom I shared the dorm.

I like my new job, my new uniform splashed with color and gongs but unsplashed, any more, with blood, and certainly not sweat because I have no intention of working for a living.

1☆15. IRON AGE FORTY-FISCATIONS

The diminutive bald man with the black cloak and heavy boots sat down on the stone steps and sighed from the bottom of his oversized paunch.

"It's no good, I can't overlook this. I would be pilloried."

The tall man with the magnificent tresses, leather jerkin, skin-tight hose and generous gusset remained standing, aloof, keeping the distance between their respective noses at well over three feet.

"But it's insignificant," he argued with more than a touch of disdain in his voice, "a spit in the Seven Seas, a pea in the garden of life."

Hairless picked his nose.

"You don't understand, my Lord. It's not just a matter of degree, though that certainly enters into it. I mean, if you'd stuck to the regulations and used the maximum forty allowed, then there'd have been no problem. But, by my reckoning, there's over eighty iron studs in that door."

Longlocks fingered his broadsword.

"Understand, sir, that I am entrusted with the defence of a hundred miles of coast. If I fail, then our world will disappear and our culture will become extinct."

Bigboots countered, pulling a parchment out from under his cloak.

"Yes, yes, of course. You've done a splendid job with the ramparts, everybody says so, but it clearly states here, look, that you're only allowed to use natural materials, stone, wood and anything else you can garner that doesn't need artificial processing. All gold, silver and iron belongs to the Crown. Them's the rules."

Skintight arched his back, stretching the septum distance to three-foot-six.

"In my defence, sir, our enemies have no such rules. They have iron weapons. That door, sir, must withstand multiple axe blows. The studs deflect them, so iron is a natural material to use against them."

Fatbelly waved the vellum two feet below the elevated nostrils.

"Be that as it may, my Liege, but I have to enforce the law, or where would any of us be? However, there may be a fiscal solution here, because subsection twenty-eight of paragraph fourteen of the Ordinance allows me to impose a tax in lieu of taking the iron away with me, providing, of course, that the breach has already occurred and is not merely one of future intent."

Broadsword sniffed the air. Was that black powder on the wind?

"Defence against attacks is my business, but in your business

I have no defence against a tax. So how am I to keep the peace?"

Shinypate scratched his head and licked his lips.

"I'll tell you what I'll do, seeing as it's only one door and you've used mortise and tenon joints in the staircase instead of nails. It's more than my life is worth, but I'll write down that there are forty studs on the outside, that will bring you within the legal limit, and I'll ignore the lock and the hook. You put ten firkins in my wagon and we'll call it a day. What do you say to that?"

Generous gusset gave no outward sign of compliance, but lifted his eyes towards the horizon, wondering whether he'd seen a sail.

1☆16. CAPO

"That's the great thing about a capo, gives you control man, lets you play any song in any key, at any pitch, just by clipping it on over them frets."

"What about America?"

"Sure, why not, which one you talking about? Horse with no name? No problem. Piece of piss. Used to play that one when I was just a kid in short trousers. Voice hadn't broken then, of course, so I'd plonk that capo right up high and stretch my little pinkies as far as they'd go, pressing on them strings as hard as I could while strumming away with my hard-bitten nails. As my voice dropped to a lower pitch I just slid that capo back down, fret by fret."

"No, I meant what about playing some gigs in America?"

"Wow, that'd be great. We could start in New York, home of The Velvet Underground. Hey, we could even play in the underground or whatever it's called over there, like we've done here, only we'd make far more dosh than the measly buggers coming off the Tube give us. We could even play Heroin, that'd go down well. Oh, and then on to Chicago to cover some Smashing Pumpkins hits, what's that one, the song about the place where you were born? Tonight? Yeah, let's do that. I reckon I could pick that one up in my sleep."

"I think I may have found us a tour promoter."

"Get away! Man, that'd be cool. I can see it now, it'd only take us a few weeks and we'd be famous, get our names up in lights. Hey we'd have some strange days out there, we could hire ourselves a tour bus and pick up some chicks from those totty-rich bars, can't see any reason why not, I mean, come on, look at us."

"You'd be happy to up sticks for the summer then?"

"Hell yes, why ever not? Can't think why we'd have any cause for regrets on that score. It'd be a doddle. Let's wander over to Frank's and talk to the boys, see their faces light up when we tell 'em. Garth's gonna wet himself."

"You'll let me tell them first? Put it gently like? Make a case?"

"You, me, what does it matter? It's a great idea we've had here. You can open if you want, but I'll pick it up and sing it loud and pretty, just like I always do. You have your pitch, then I'll have mine and we'll bring 'em along, just like we always do. Your pitch then mine."

"You'll be needing your capo then."

1☆17. UNSETTLED

He could feel it. Just the tiniest movement, under his feet, but he could definitely feel it. A wave of irritation crept up his legs, through his stomach and lodged in his throat as a distinct lump. He breathed deeply, trying to control what he knew was coming next. He closed his eyes to block out the light but it had no effect. Within seconds the flash burned the back of his eyelids and blanked out everything else. He dropped to the floor and scrunched immediately into a foetal position, pulling his knees up to his chin and screwing his fingers into fists. His chest muscles went into spasm. Now he couldn't breathe at all. Time stopped.

When he woke, he stared in disbelief and despair at the destruction. Nothing remained upright. The table was upturned in a corner, a detached leg hanging limply from a jagged hole in the shiplap wall. The futon mattress had taken the door off its hinges and now lay doubled up outside on the sand. Tea stained the wooden floor, making uneven patterns around shattered pieces of crockery. The chair was missing and torn curtains flapped outwards through the broken window. He had blood on his hands.

His first attack had come out of the blue when he was thirty. Then his wife had tried to understand, had sought the best medical help, had put her trust fund to work with the wisest counsellors and the latest drugs. But they kept coming. Every insignificant imbalance in his life brought devastation out of all proportion. There had to be a limit. Within five years the foundations of his life had crumbled and he was divorced, jobless and homeless. He knew he was lucky to have his freedom but feared that he would soon lose that if he stayed in the world he now found both intolerant and intolerable. So he left.

The changing climate had been a friend, allowing a life on the beach where the waves and tides brought a new rhythm, a calming cadence that pushed his anger into memory. He made friends with the fishermen who said he brought them luck. Out on the ocean, in their boats, the rocking movement under his feet felt natural and he grew strong and confident again.

He enjoyed the banter as they sat mending nets. Irreverent and humorous, it gave him a sense of equilibrium. But then there were more and more questions about why he slept on the sand, an impermanent, shifting existence. In some strange way it made them feel uncomfortable. He began to sense the tension again and agreed, under pressure, to settle into one of the huts along the shoreline.

He didn't want clutter, it would overwhelm him, just a table and a chair and a light mattress, a teapot and one cup. He took the lock off the door. More than security, what he wanted was stability. The fishermen were pleased to see their protégé respond in this way. They understood. Their own stability came from the pulse of the sea, a steady unsteadiness under their feet that flowed through their lives.

The huts were simple wooden constructions, bolted down onto concrete screeds. No especial care had been taken and here and there the cement had powdered in the salty air. Not a problem; no great shakes. But this morning, after he had made an early pot of tea and was pulling on a T-shirt, one of those inconsequential crumblings created the smallest cavity under a two-by-four post and the screed moved, a minuscule fraction of an inch. An invisible crack crazed out from one side of the post, then zig-zagged in slow steps across the concrete floor. He could feel it. Just the tiniest movement, under his feet, but he could definitely feel it.

1☆18. GRAVESEND QUARRY

We always played there when we were kids. Of course, we were told not to, far too dangerous for squirts like us. But we, by that I mean *he*, had the rabbit's foot. Tiny Terry, not an inch over four foot, and he was 'fraid of nothin', because he had the lucky charm. He could swim right across the quarry in his clothes, climb out and still run the pants off the rest of us, laughing all the way.

It was a present from his grandad, so he said, who survived the worst of war with nary a scratch on him while the others in his squad were picked off one by one, sniper, mortar, landmine and even dysentery. So Terry was untouchable and his luck rubbed off on the rest of us.

Until the greasers came, their triumphant pipes thundering and their tyres criss-crossing our secret tracks, throwing up mud over our fire and gouging channels through our camp. We scarpered into the gorse bushes, scratched our pride and hid. Except Terry. He ran out with his arms windmilling above his head, shouting at them to fuck off.

Fuck off they did, but only after they'd lifted little Terry onto the handlebars of a bike and rode off with him swearing.

He came back an hour later, his clothes torn and his face blackened, but his eyes bright.

"I showed 'em," he bragged. "They won't be back here

again."

We heard about it on Sugg's pocket radio. Tragic accident. He was only seventeen they said. Funeral on Saturday. No flowers.

That's when Terry started frantically searching his pockets.

"Shit!"

"What's the matter?" we asked.

"My rabbit's foot. It's gone."

We searched for whole day, kicking over the clumps of gravelly mud, gingerly parting the gorse.

"That bastard must have taken it," said Terry. "We've got to get it back."

So we went to the funeral to mingle and mystify his family, only Terry wasn't with us, without his rabbit's foot he was too scared. But we tilted our heads down and pricked up our ears and we listened. Born to ride…. Loved that bike…. Buried in full leathers….

Later that night, back at the quarry, we told Terry.

"It'll be in his pocket. You gotta get it back for me. You gotta dig him up. You gotta."

Well of course we didn't. Quarry's gone now, filled in. Houses built around. Village became town became suburbs. More people, more deaths. Some of the graves from the old cemetery are being moved to make room. Terry's a newspaper man now, covers all the hard luck stories in the town, so he hears about these things. Says he knows exactly where that bastard is going to be buried again, has it marked on a map, and this time he'll be waiting.

1☆19. BUT NOT YET!

Her eyes catch mine and I get an instant boner. There's no feeling like it. My blood is running like Niagara, tipping me over the edge and pumping up my heart until I hear the barrel organs in my brain thump against my skull.

Bang, bang, bang.

When I was a kid, I watched Apollo 11 take off and I nearly wet my pants with excitement. But that was like eating candyfloss compared to this. Sweet and sickly against this sour but irresistibly exhilarating taste in my mouth now that swims around my tongue.

Suck, suck, suck.

Her eighteen-year-old body curves around my imagination like a serpent, slipping in and out of my desire, like consciousness on the cusp of nirvana. My nerves are prickling like pins and needles, driving a pulsing rhythm up and down my limbs.

Throb, throb, throb.

My slithery palms drop sweat on the Book as I stand in the pulpit and I wipe them on my cassock, feeling the electric potential as my skin glides across the polyester sheen. She's still looking, staring at my face, my façade of holiness.

Lord, Lord, Lord.

Make me good…

Please!

…but not yet!

1☆20. GRANMARDI GRAS

Today was going to be one hell of a day.

Estelle, born on the 8th March, 1911, had been planning it for five years. Rising even before the sun had cracked the curtains, she had run her daily bath and lifted her legs over the edge, one by one, and braced herself for her constitutional dipping as her granddaughter came in to hang a towel on the radiator.

"Geeeezzzzzzz! That water's freezing," shrieked Millie, whipping her hand out of the bath and running it immediately under the hot tap in the basin. "You'll catch your death."

"Don't be such a wuss. How do you think I've stayed fit all my life? Cold baths, that's how Houdini did it. Now he was a real man, there's no escaping that. Anyway, after today it wouldn't be so bad if I moved on. I've done my time and been a pain in the arse for too many people to be forgotten."

In the bedroom, Rosalind picked up the purple, green and white striped Two Piece on the chair and gasped. "She's really going to do it. Oh my god, that means I've got to do it too. No chance of getting out of it now." Rosalind knew her mother only too well and after seventy years of intransigence was too afraid to try talking her out of it, muttering instead her misgivings out loud to herself. "If I put my foot down now, we'd end up killing each other."

Estelle bundled Millie out of the way, ignoring the proffered towel and took determined steps towards Rosalind.

"What you staring at? Haven't you seen anyone naked before?"

Both Rosalind and Millie had, of course, but seeing a centenarian with no clothes is like watching a re-run of ET. As if on cue, Estelle stretched her shoulders back and lifted her wrinkled head before snatching the swimsuit out of Rosalind's hands.

"I'm set. What are you two going to wear?"

Rosalind blushed and offered, "well, I thought my new jersey would be nice."

"Just make sure you can roll it up when the time comes."

Millie retrieved hot pants and a boob tube from her suitcase and dangled them in front of Estelle. A confident thirty-year-old, she was looking forward to showing off with the razzamatazz her grandmother had talked about five years ago.

Estelle remembered too. Her eyes were on fire, as they had been in 1914 when, on only her third birthday, she had been with her mother on the march from Bow to Trafalgar Square. Raised on equality since that first International Women's Day on 8th March 1911, Estelle embraced the notion with a willing eagerness. She'd only married Robert because war had been declared and, even then, showed considerably less enthusiasm for that other thing that men did and which resulted in Rosalind's birth in 1940.

Thereafter, Rosalind had been taken by her mother from meeting to convention and, by the time she was a young woman, had unquestioningly accepted the inevitability of equal rights. Even when she fancied the pants off Donovan Court, she held out against wedlock on her mother's insistence, until that long hot summer of 1975 when Donovan, to the strains of Neil Young, had finally charmed the pants off her and they thought they had better tie the knot, just in case anything happened. Happen it did, but not until five years later when, as Rosalind then argued, Britain had a Queen *and* a woman prime minister so we could all relax a little.

When Millie arrived in the autumn of 1980, she relaxed naturally into the world and grew up regarding equality as her birthright. To prove her inherited independence, she moved to America immediately after graduating, leaving her mother and grandmother behind. Working in an ad agency where the average age was under thirty, she soon settled into the belief that old people were dull, almost irrelevant. Her attitude changed during her last visit over the pond in 2006. That's when Estelle shocked her with her vivacity and resolution and the plot was hatched.

Now here was the day, Mardi Gras, 8th March 2011, the centenary of International Women's Day and Estelle's 100th birthday.

As the bands blew their ears off and the crowds pushed along Bourbon Street, Rosalind and Millie stalked slowly on either side of Estelle, up to the balconies of ivy-strung beads.

Taking a firm grip on the lower hem of her top, Estelle elbowed her escorts out of her way and shouted to the revellers above, "Are you ready?"

1☆21. PROMPTED BLINDNESS

Isaac ran his fingers over the apple. It felt warm and soft. He imagined he could feel the colors, a ripe russet on one side and a pale yellow-green on the other where it had been turned away from the sun. He should have turned away, but then what would he have learned?

His mother should have turned away from the Reverend, but she would never learn.

The darkened room opened up a new world for Isaac, a new sense of touch for a young man untouched by love or kindness. The prism now, cold, angular and sharp in his hands, refracted in his mind's eye and cast a rainbow shadow over his visionary determination.

1☆22. AURORA

It must be, what, nearly forty years ago now. My memory of circumstances is not what it used to be, but I seem to recall that it wasn't too long after I spent that memorable night at Maud's house.

Back then, my friends, such as they were, teased me constantly about my love life, and I can tell you are about to do the same. But no, Maud was an inspiration to me. We made conversation, not love.

This did not satisfy those in my close circle. "What is the point" asked Vidal, "of being a rich eligible bachelor if you do not exploit your opportunities?"

"What makes you think I do not?" I would reply, "Opportunity can be seen in areas other than sexual exploration." Vidal would raise and lower his eyebrows, feigning surprise and disapproval almost at the same time, unsure as he was of how to take my remarks.

Aurora, with the sensitivities of a woman writer, should have understood but, if anything, she was more irritating than Vidal. She did not believe I could spend an entire night with a beautiful woman without coaxing a tête-à-tête into the goose feathers. If I were not so frustrated with her, I would laugh, but she pressed me where it hurt most.

Therefore, I determined to have it out with her, to put my

philosophy in such words that her eyes would be opened and she would see our fellow humans as I did. And if not, then I would just have to keep my distance during our conversations. With this quest in my heart, I drove down to her house in the French Alps. The journey in the mountain airs buoyed my spirits and I was in good humour when I arrived, so that even the sight of Vidal walking out onto the terrace could not throw doubts into my resolve.

I was greeted by Gilbert, who carried my case up to my room.

"Madame is resting," he said quietly.

"A heavy lunch?" I asked lightly.

"Yes sir."

"You are discreet as always, Gilbert, I will tiptoe down to the terrace after I've changed out of these travelling clothes."

"As you wish, sir. I will have a chilled beer waiting for you." He nodded and turned in the way of an old retainer who accepted the world without question.

Vidal had the backgammon board out and was fingering the dice lazily.

"There you are Jérôme, I was beginning to think that I should have to spend all afternoon playing with myself. Will you have a game?"

"It is not my ideal method of relaxation after a long drive, but if you must." I sat down beside him, catching his heavy animal scent on the air.

"Well, if you prefer, I can offer you another game…" His eyes glanced at me sideways, the mischief shooting out from under half-closed lids.

My mood stayed positive. I was here to talk to Aurora, but Vidal was never far away from my host and lived, almost permanently, as her house-guest. I decided to humour him until Aurora had rested and I could reasonably make my excuses to go and find her. I did not realise that events would bring that moment closer.

"What is this game?" I said.

"Our mutual friend is drunk." Vidal was always blunt. "She's up in her room right now sleeping it off. Of course, I tried to keep her sober, but the thought of you coming this afternoon seemed to make her nervous and one glass followed another, as it does…"

"I'm sure she was simply bored with your company."

"Touché! I might almost say ouch, but it's what I expect of you these days. Tell me, how is Maud?"

"Delightful as always. Now what is this game?"

He looked directly at me. The corners of his mouth turned up, ever so slightly, but his eyes were not smiling as they wandered over my face, looking for clues as to my state of mind.

"I will throw a die and, if it lands on a six, you will go up to Aurora's room and make love to her."

His eyes narrowed further as the tension showed in the muscles of my cheeks. I tried to fake indifference as I answered him, "It was never my belief that we should be frivolous with our friends, but sincere and respectful in our approach towards each other. God does not play dice."

He laughed, a hollow chuckle that made me feel diminished. At the same time, he rolled a die and laughed again when it fell six up.

"There's your God, telling you as clear as clear can be what you should do now, if you dare."

The blood rose up through my tight collar, swelling my veins and turning my face dark. I could not stay here with him a minute longer, so I stood and left without another word.

I climbed the stairs to my room, intent on lying down until my composure returned, but as I walked past Aurora's door, I heard her sigh.

"Are you alright, Aurora?" No answer, she must be sleeping, but I turned the handle and pushed the door open, the better to hear her if she said anything.

"Are you awake?" Her muffled answer sounded disturbed, so I entered the room.

She lay on her back on the bed with her feet on the floor, her shoes kicked off and her light summer dress lying gently on her legs. The window was open and I sat on a chair beside it, to catch the cooling breeze. I watched her breathing, her lips exhaling half-words, and her breast rising and falling softly with her dream. Her knees were spread a little apart and she looked like a child who had fallen asleep after playing in the garden, clothed with exhaustion and innocence.

I leaned forward and put my hand on her knee; holding it gently. Then I stood, bowed my head over hers and kissed her lightly on the cheek. She stirred but did not wake.

Gilbert carried my case down to the car.

"Leaving so soon sir?"

"I've just remembered some business in Lyon I must attend to."

Over my shoulder, I caught a final triumphant glare from Vidal and the gravel crunched as I drove off towards Maud's house.

☆☆☆☆☆☆☆☆☆☆☆☆☆☆☆☆☆☆☆☆

THE STORIES - VOL.2

☆☆☆☆☆☆☆☆☆☆☆☆☆☆☆☆☆☆☆☆

2☆1. THE PEDANT'S WIFE

Jorge collapsed clumsily onto a bench in the Placa de George Orwell, in the old quarter of the bewildering metropolis that to him was Barcelona. His own bulk was outweighed only by the heaviness in his mind. His confusion leaked out of his pores as he sweated under the relentless afternoon sun. What was he to do now?

The memory of the lawyer's face glared at him from the back of his eyelids, and he could still hear the voice in his ears, cold and passionless.

"Do you understand Senor Sanchez?"

Jorge had sat motionless in the dusty office, fussy with files half-seen in the dim light behind closed blinds.

"Your father has left you the farm, Senor, for five years…"

Five years? What did that mean? Five long hot summers, five bitterly cold winters?

"After that, it will pass to your cousin, your father's brother's son."

His cousin, Federico, was a distant memory, unvisiting and unvisited since he was a child.

"Unless, by then, you are married with your own son, an

heir."

Married with a son? Him, Jorge Sanchez? How was he going to find a wife and have a son in just five years? He knew nothing of women. His mother had died in childbirth. All of his father's considerable experience in lambing had been useless when it came to saving a human being. He hadn't seen his father's humour and laughter before that day, when he came into the world, and his mother left it. All he had known was bitterness and silence. The only tenderness he had learned was towards the sheep and his dogs. Now, at the age of forty-four, how was he going to find a wife?

Slowly Jorge wiped a cotton handkerchief across his brow and down over his face. He opened his eyes and blinked, as if trying to adjust to a strange new world. He'd never been to Barcelona before and had travelled the long miles from the farm with a naïve curiosity that now turned into a morbid fear in his stomach. The noises bounced around inside his head and the bright colours all around contrasted sharply with the endless browns of home.

A movement caught his eye and he turned his head sideways to see a young woman kneeling down on the rough cobbles by the side of the street. She had long black hair and was wearing a scarlet dress, with a white lace shawl over her shoulders. A Prada bag rested in her lap and she was rustling through it with intense concentration. After a minute, she took out a ball of string.

The string pulled Jorge's mind back to the farm and an unwritten list of a thousand jobs he still had to tackle. He should be moving on, getting home, but his exhaustion kept him slumped on the bench. He watched the woman for at least five minutes before realising that she *was* a woman. Young and beautiful, like his neighbour's daughters who giggled and disappeared inside whenever they saw him ride up on his trail bike to talk to their father about the heat, the drought, the fencing repairs or a lame ewe.

Whether he could find a wife at all was already too high a mountain for Jorge to climb in his mind, but even if he did, he was convinced she wouldn't be young and beautiful. More like the Widow Cervantes, with her tobacco breath and broken teeth. She could cook a mean mutton stew and handle a pair of shears, but she was past child-bearing age and there'd be no heir from her.

Jorge sighed and let his head fall backwards. What was that up on the post? A camera? What was that for? The lawyer's voice came back to him.

"It is important you understand Senor Sanchez, the conditions of your father's will are exact and must be upheld. Do not think that you can go back to the farm and forget about them. We will be watching you."

All his childhood years he had wanted someone to watch over him, but his mother was dead and his father didn't seem to care where he was, so he had spent his time up in the hills with the flock. Now everyone was dead and this lawyer was watching him? He didn't understand. All of a sudden, it was too strange a world.

The woman, he noticed, was tying the string round a red bicycle propped up against a lamp post. Not just round one part of it, but round all of it, teasing the string out of the ball as she went. She tied the wheels, the spokes, the pedals, the upright, the diagonal bar, the handlebar. Suddenly, Jorge could stand no more confusion.

"What are you doing?" he asked.

The woman seemed startled, as if in a deep reverie.

"Who, me?" she said.

"Yes, you. What are you doing? Why are you tying all that string round that bicycle?"

"Ha ha," she laughed lightly. Then turned back to her task as if this was a private joke, but after she tied a final knot, she dusted her hands together and stood up.

"There," she said, "that'll take him at least an hour."

Jorge watched her put the ball of string back in the bag.

"Take who an hour? I don't understand."

Now the young woman turned and looked Jorge in the eye. She was truly beautiful, he thought.

"Why my husband, of course. That's his bicycle. Well, it's mine really, but he always takes it to work." She pointed behind Jorge. "Over there, in that building." Jorge did not turn round but carried on staring at the woman. He noticed the pleats in her red dress, how they hung like the curtains at home.

She laughed again and, as if making a condescending decision, walked over to Jorge and sat down beside him on the bench. He could smell her perfume.

"My husband is a strange man. Of course, I didn't know that when I married him, but when you live with someone, you find out all sorts of things you couldn't imagine otherwise."

Jorge couldn't imagine living with this young woman.

"He's handsome and has a good job and looks after me well, but underneath all that he's a bit of a crackpot. No, that's unfair, he's a…" she looked up and to the right, "a pedant, that's what he is."

"A pedant?" After all the legal words Jorge had heard that morning, this one struggled to the front of the queue for understanding.

"You know," she said as she smiled, "someone who is pernickety, who just has to get every little thing right, someone who looks at the details all the time."

Jorge thought of his father taking the truck's carburettor apart, all the tiny pieces on the kitchen table. The truck never went again.

"I'm Teodora, by the way, and my husband, Alvar, is a man who cannot let a challenge go by without picking it to bits. He's going to go nuts when he sees his bike. He'll know it was me and, because of that, he will have to outdo me by untying every single knot." She laughed again, but this time heartily, with her head thrown back, showing her long neck to Jorge. He felt the sweat dripping down inside his shirt. Was everyone in this city crazy?

"Why?"

"Why what?"

"Why would you want to do such a thing?"

"Why not? It makes me laugh to think of him kneeling down here in his best suit, scuffing his polished shoes, breaking his manicured fingernails, swearing under his breath, trying to untie all this string." As she spoke, her eyes sparkled and her right hand inadvertently shot up to pull an ebony tress over the back of her ear.

"I don't understand," Jorge shook his head, his own black mane tumbling unkempt down over broad shoulders, "I don't understand anything anymore. I'm just a simple man."

She leaned backwards, as if to get a better look at Jorge, running her eyes up and down his large but strong frame, his tanned and muscular forearms, his unshaven craggy face. Her lips closed tightly together while she smiled widely, breathing in noisily through her nose as she did so, pulling her shoulders up and back before letting them fall in a half-shrug.

"Yes, I think you are. Right now, though, I'd give almost anything to be married to a simple man."

Her resignation complete, she stood again and offered her hand to Jorge, who remained sitting.

"Good bye my simple man. I'll bet you have a much happier life than my husband."

Jorge shook her hand lightly, then watched, still confused, as she picked up her bag and sashayed down the street, with the air and composure of a catwalk model.

After another five minutes, Jorge himself stood. He stretched, a long high stretch, then reached down to his own bag and pulled out a pair of sheep shears. Life was too complicated, he thought, then walked over to the bicycle and cut the strings.

2☆2. "HELLO WORLD"

"Good morning Brian."

"Morning Dennis."

"You done any more work on that Unix O/S?"

"Shed loads."

"Anything interesting?"

"You bet your sweet arse. What would you say to a long int data type AND an unsigned int data type?"

"You're joking! You never!"

"Yup, I did. What's more, I've changed the compound assignment operators to remove the semantic ambiguity."

"Fuck, no!"

"Sure did."

"Gee, and there was I getting all excited about a standard I/O library."

"And I've thrown out all that crap about function arguments and parameters."

"How on earth did you manage that?"

"I cheated and swapped them for warning messages."

"Hell man, what's ANSI going to make of all this?"

"Do we care?"

"'I guess not, seeing that what we've come up with can make arbitrary use of whitespace to format code."

"That's what I was thinking."

"Reckon we'll make any money out of this?"

"Does it matter?"

2☆3. THE FREEDOM

My name is Cal White. I'm a happy, well-grounded farmer and life just couldn't be better. Tomorrow, all of us here who share the fruits of the earth are going to celebrate that feeling, because tomorrow is the 500th anniversary of The Freedom. That's our Freedom I'm talking about, not theirs, not the Cielists', though who knows they may be celebrating their Freedom up there wherever they are.

Five hundred years is a long time, too long for most of us to imagine, but we know that it's taken every one of those years to get life back to normality. It's been hard work and we have our milestones in history by which to remember. The date now is 31st December 10,999 STE so tomorrow is also the beginning of the 12th millennia. The Cielists had their own time and would have said this year is 2999 CE, but we've used STE since The Freedom and it's good enough for us.

I still find it difficult to fathom, that for over four and a half billion years, life evolved out of the earth and found it a good life, worth living and celebrating, yet in just a few thousand years of highfalutin sky worship we took our feet off the ground and lost our way. Looking back over the Cielists' stories, you could see it coming. Their heroes were always looking upwards. The Wright Brothers and Yuri Gagarin took the first physical steps to lift heads literally into the clouds, but when Eve Sequoia and Carlos Mendocino returned from their fanciful voyage to another galaxy, the madness took hold in an unstoppable wave of excitement. One hundred years, they said, a century to prepare for departure and then their great grandchildren would embrace The Freedom.

Well good riddance to them I say, as do all of us who are still here, descended from the handful of sensible people who stayed behind. So we call it The Freedom as well; freedom from all those crazy ideas that broke down the sense of wholeness that we now value above everything else. There's not a day goes by without me picking up a handful of soil and letting it run through my fingers, knowing that there are billions of living things in it, and remembering that it's where I came from too. Yes me, and my kids, Kanona, Katahdin, Kennebec and Krantz (everyone calls them the ForKs), and my neighbours Russet Norking and Red LaSoda, and all the other people in our local enclampment. We know the earth is where we came from and where we will end up when we die.

Only the other day, Norland was telling me his crop has never been so healthy since his mother, old Shepody, was composted. Of course we all grieved for a month, gathering round and supporting him, but it's natural and he's got his son Norwis to think of, taking his seed forwards, and he knows that when his time comes he will be helping him in the same way.

When the Cielists took off, they left us with the technology to remember the past. We still keep the old information and use it to understand what went wrong, which is helpful in a way I suppose. But they also left us with a dead planet and that's what's taken us five hundred years to sort out. My great, great grandfather wrote in his Deathbook about his worries that we wouldn't make it in time for tomorrow. That's how far ahead we think these days, but we have succeeded and when Pike and Sebago carry the tubers to the new Millenium

Farm for Monona to plant in the best soil we've ever known, it will mark a true Freedom.

2☆4. PGAD

Is that thing switched on? Shall I just talk?

OK.

It started about two years ago. I'd been taking some antidepressants for about a week and then I noticed these hot flushes. Didn't think too much about them at first, but then I began to feel strong vibrations. I mean, if I was on a train and the carriage juddered, as it sometimes does, I'd get a spasm in my vagina. It was quite gentle at first, but after another week it was all I could do to stifle my gasps because I'd be coming over and over again.

Oh… Ah… Oh…

Sorry.

My boyfriend thought it was his birthday and Christmas coming together, no pun intended, because he only had to take his boxers off and I'd be on the floor holding my fanny. Quite literally groaning. But it wasn't long before he got pissed off. I think he felt sort of left out, because I'd be having orgasms continuously with or without him. Even the hairdryer would set me off.

Nnnnmmmmm. Aaaagggh.

Sorry again.

Anyway I went to the doctor and she said I had this rare medical condition called PGAD - Persistent Genital Arousal Disorder. Yes, seriously, I'm not joking. Apparently it increases the blood flow to my sex organs, making them hypersensitive. They respond to almost any vibration. I even have to be careful when using the photocopier because I know they're all staring at me, waiting for it to start. They think it's funny but I'm getting heartily fed up with it all. I mean, can you imagine having up to two hundred orgasms a day?

Ahhhhhhh. Uuuunnng.

So sorry.

Please don't laugh. You might think it amusing, but this PGAD thing is ruining my life. I'm worn out. I can't sleep unless I have at least a dozen climaxes and I can't keep a boyfriend long enough to do that every single night. So I put on a robe, go downstairs, and sit on the spin dryer for ten minutes.

Gggnnnnnnnn.

Oh, I do apologize, have you got enough now? I have to be somewhere. I think I'll catch the five o'clock train, but there's something I have to do first.

2☆5. TREEBOUND

It took me fifteen years to work out what had happened.

In the beginning, everything was hazy, like staring into thick fog. Only after five years did this cloud thin enough to allow a diffused light to penetrate, like mist rising off a river. Even then, I was only aware of vague outlines and indefinite shapes.

After ten years, the memories began to return, in two dimensions at first, but gaining depth as each further anniversary passed: an event, an horrendous occurrence, an irreversible fate.

Over this last year, I've seen pastel colours passing and heard grumblings getting louder then softer. Then it goes dark and I wait for the pairs of eyes to shine at me before they run away, always off to the left.

But yesterday, they didn't turn and they didn't run. They kept coming, brighter and brighter, the grumbling louder and louder. Then a loud bang and a sharp pain as the eyes closed and the sound changed to a hissing.

This morning, I am not alone; a young woman has joined me. She's unconscious, unknowing, unaware of what happened. Will it take her fifteen years? She has a rather sad feel to her, but I'll take care of her, look after her, until she's ready.

This tree is comfortable enough, has plenty of room, and has become a rather special home.

2☆6. A MONETARY CRISIS

The trouble started when the Royal Mint announced that it simply couldn't meet the production needs of the new notes in time. So much for forward planning. We'd had years to decide whether to join the rest of Europe and now it had to happen yesterday. The Minister for Currency spent twenty-four hours on the phone to his counterparts in France, Germany, Italy and Spain, but they declined to assist, explaining that inflation had already reduced their stocks below the mandatory reserves.

"Je suis désolé, mais il est impossible…."

"Es tut mir leid, mein freund, aber…."

"Mi dispiace…."

"Lo siento…."

To prevent a national disaster, the Prime Minister intervened with Orders in Council that allowed an extension of the Credit Act to cover everyday purchases. The Chancellor of the Exchequer announced that the recently privatised banks would honour debit card balances up to a value equivalent to a month's salary for each citizen. But somehow that didn't seem to help. Public confidence plummeted and alternative trade schemes sprang out of back rooms to be tested on street corners. Cigarettes were no longer smoked, but exchanged for groceries, clothes, and other necessities. The black market, with its own hierarchy, suddenly became a serious threat to law and order.

In the City, money brokers frantically sold futures and invented new hedge products linked to commodities, coffee, sugar, oil, wheat and, of course, gold.

"This is better than war," they chorused, "we'll break the government on this one."

In the basement of New Scotland Yard, the Commissioner was taking a verbal beating from a Home Office mandarin.

"The situation is the worst we've known since Bretton Woods. The banks are under a sustained attack from organised crime and our entire economy is at risk. We can hold the line, for now, by accommodating international trade agreements with promissory notes and reciprocal assurances, but here at home people will starve if we can't find the liquidity to move goods freely around the country. Insurrection is on lips everywhere. And you, Sir Nigel, have to stop that happening."

So the big wheels started turning. Secret conferences pushed papers in red boxes to rapidly formed committees that stamped, signed and counter-signed fresh orders and plans which, in turn, were couriered to Chief Constables in every region. The battle was on. Human resources were diverted from vice and traffic to expanded fraud squads as every form of credit manipulation was anticipated. Even the purge on money laundering was allowed to slide in favour of a heightened focus on speculative theft and notional shoplifting, from the internet all the way down to street level.

That's how I came to be involved, Detective Inspector Bill Tally. I wasn't sorry to get out of the dismal daily chore of chasing pimps and their sad protégés around the back alleys of Paddington but I hadn't expected to swap a difficult task for an impossible one.

"Let me get this straight," I asked my Super, "you want me to monitor the slates being chalked up in all the pubs, clubs and betting shops from Hillingdon to Havering, and from Barnet to Bromley, then track down and lock up anyone who exceeds a salary-based credit limit or who, by the end of the month, fails to settle up in full?"

"That's it in a nutshell I'm afraid. It's the informal and unregistered sources of credit that are the most dangerous, so we have little choice; we have to keep a lid on this thing." The tired expression on his face said more, but he wasn't going to endanger his pension by telling me.

"I'll be the laughing stock of the Met. It's bad enough my team hauling half-clothed prostitutes down stairs to the cells, but collaring hypothetical blaggers who default on their tabs will have the boys in blue sniggering behind my back."

"I'm sorry Bill, but with your experience you're the best man for the job. I'll see you get all the support you need."

And with that he stood up and left the room, closing the glass-panelled door on which was painted my new title, "Chief of Currency Shortage Credit Control."

Underneath it, in permanent black marker, some wise ass had already scribbled: *"N.EuroTick Policeman."*

2☆7. CHEMISTRY SET

When it happened, it was just one of those unfortunate industrial accidents: I caught my finger in the jigsaw and before I could even feel the pain, my upturned digit was on the floor colouring the sawdust around it bright red. They managed to sew it back on again, but it never quite took and a month later it was in a pickle jar. I keep it on the workbench where I can see it moving up and down in the liquid, a nagging reminder to be careful.

But careful is a foreign word to a youngster full of the spirit of life. In less than a year I had signed up for one of those insane expeditions for charity, a supposedly simple trek to a relatively safe Himalayan base camp. That's how they described it, but I still managed to leave two of my toes up there after a severe attack of frostbite.

Then last month I was back on the operating table having my appendix out. Recovering in the ward with time on my hands, or most of them, so to speak, I started to run through a limb and organ count of what I had left. If I had used my fingers and toes, then I'd have been limited to seventeen at a time. That's when it struck me how much of my body I had been losing over the years.

As a baby I'd left my foreskin in the Mount Sinai hospital. Never knew it, never missed it. My milk teeth disappeared one by one from under my pillow to the lair of the tooth fairy. Made a small profit on those.

Then there was all that hair I had left on the barber's floor, to be swept up without a moment's thought by the maestro's assistant. After that, it was finger and toenail clippings. Even with my numerical handicap, it must have amounted to several bucketfuls. And what about all those skin cells rubbed off at night onto the sheets, to be washed and rinsed down the drain to wherever? And talking of sheets, there was all that bodily fluid I'd been spilling since puberty.

They say that you are what you eat, or, more accurately, what you digest, so there's several hundred bathtub equivalents of faeces and urine I've donated to the sewage system. And I was a chubby teenager before I started playing basketball, so I think I can add at least thirty pounds of fat to the list. I have no idea where that might be now, but I'm not carrying it around anymore.

By the time the nurse came with my medication, I felt less like a person than a cellular processing plant, a chemistry set on legs, leaking as I walked, and even as I sat there in bed breaking out in a sweat at the thought that I was melting away. I would have cried, but I didn't want to make it worse.

I've forgotten about it all now. I don't miss my finger or toes; I can still play basketball and a fairly mean game of soccer. If I lose a pound or two through sweat in a particularly energetic session, then that's OK. If my cells die, on average, every seven years and end up somehow in the municipal dump, to be recycled into compost or paper bags, then I just imagine that I'm doing my bit for ecology.

So I'll continue to scatter my body wherever I go, with philosophical abandon.

2☆8. MATRICIDE

"They lied to us."

The voice was low and rumbled like a muffled drum a mile away, reaching the ear as thunder on a cyclonic evening, an ominous threat of worse to come.

Flynn opened his eyes and they immediately filled with brine in the lightning glare of the O.R. halogens. He wanted to wipe them but his arms lay still beside him like fallen branches. Yet he could feel the breath in his nostrils and the slow rise and fall of his chest.

"You're back with us. Don't worry, sensation will return soon."

The storm moved closer. He could feel the cold rustle of cloth beside his face, teasing his hair with static. He stretched his fingers, stiff like twigs, scratching the starched bed linen.

His vision began to clear, enough to catch the outline of two figures.

"Everything will seem different. You won't know who you are. You mustn't panic, or the chemical stress will affect the final stages of reformatting. Waking in peace is essential."

The silhouettes were moving, but the words were now inside his head, colouring in his feelings; reds, blues, yellows, greens.

He became aware of his nakedness and, with superhuman effort, he inched his hands over to his groin. There was no penis, no manhood.

"They all do that. It's the first shock, but relax, the matrices are still balancing, returning to their origins."

Flynn tried to speak, but the words eddied in his throat as a breezy sigh and the only sound that emerged was the rustle of wet leaves.

"It'll take a day or so before you can talk again, after your oesophagus has healed. It was one of the weapons they used, speech, enshrined in the logos, the first technique of difference training."

Flynn squeezed his eyes shut, the escaping tears moistening his cheeks, running into his ears, over his lobes. He felt a most delicate sensation. What was happening, what *had* happened to him?

"Take it easy. Don't try to absorb it all too soon. Hermaphrodism was our first natural state, but returning to it will take some getting used to. We've a few million years to catch up on. Another few days won't matter."

In his head there was a clash of thunder, a mind-splitting pain, a bolt of rejection. His body shook like an electrified corpse.

"Calm down. If we lose you now, we won't be able to bring you back. That was the price, the Contract with Adam, as we call it, when the first multi-cellular organisms chose sex as the way. They unbalanced the matrices, killed our independence, brought

difference and hierarchy into the world."

Flynn felt his limbs stiffening, his muscles tightening, his mind constricting into a pinpoint of nothingness. He drifted into another place, a wilderness of thought. The words were all around his body, tickling his skin from the inside. His cells were talking to him, no, not to him, but to each other.

The eye of the storm was over her and she felt a wave of peace, a knowledge of strength returning with which to face the second half.

"You're one of us again now. We know the truth. We know they lied to us, but they can't do that anymore."

2☆9. THE IDEAL HOMO SAPIENS EXHIBITION

Frances Fenella ffarquharson took one look at the naked Olympian on display and disappeared abruptly into another world. In the physical reality of this world, a thin dribble of gin escaped from the corner of her mouth as she bit down on an olive stone, dislodging a gold crown. But she felt no pain because the tooth was in her head and her head was up there with the gods.

Her companion, Eliza, a diminutive and plainly dressed cousin from the side of the family that lost their inheritance too long ago for the reason to be remembered, except that it was a man's weakness, of course, tugged at her sleeve. Looking sideways at the small gathering of gentlewomen who fussed and blushed around the athlete, she whispered as loudly as she felt was acceptable.

"Fanny, what are you doing? Fanny, behave yourself." But Fanny didn't hear her.

Eliza caught the stem of the Waterford cocktail glass as it slipped from Fanny's fingers.

The exhibition guide responsible for the group, the Kensington Seekers of Pulchritude, knew her audience. She couldn't hope to catch their eyes, nor indeed their ears, so she spoke to their hearts.

"Ladies, I don't have to tell you, I don't have to suggest, I don't even have to intimate, because you know that before you stands a male of perfect proportions. On loan to us today by the very kind permission of the Athenian Discus Throwers Association."

Fanny's delicate tricolour bamboo sunshade bowed under her weight as her knees buckled under her imagination.

Eliza was not so affected. She slipped her arm around Fanny's eighteen-inch waist and squeezed.

"Fanny, let's go. We've seen too much already." But Fanny didn't feel her.

The guide continued. "In a few minutes time, we shall be lucky enough to witness a demonstration of muscular prowess, a sight to be wondered at and remembered for a lifetime."

Eliza frowned and pouted, pushing her painted bottom lip out and up over her cupid's bow.

"Perfect proportions my arse. Who says a man can't have one leg longer than another, or six fingers on one hand, or a cock that curves a little to the left? As long as his heart is bigger than his head and he has more guts than stomach. That's all I ask for in a man."

She set the glass down on the edge of an aspidistra stand and used her free hand to pinch the flesh between Fanny's thumb and forefinger, because that's how she used to awaken her nephew when he was deep in slumber. Fanny flinched and began to turn, but it was too late. The demonstration was beginning and a plenary gasp arose from the group.

Eliza was turning to leave just as Frances Fenella ffarquharson fainted.

2☆10. ANDERS CELSIUS

What would you have done?

My father was a professor of Astronomy and his father was a mathematician and his father-in-law was also an astronomer. With that background and upbringing I was hardly likely to become a musician, or an artist, was I? Anyway, up here in Uppsala I found precious little to do except lie on my back and stare up at the stars. That's why I travelled so much. Anywhere would do, Germany, Italy, France, just as long as it got me out of this wilderness.

How much more fun would it have been, though, if I could have journeyed to the stars, the objects of my observations? That made me think. I began to wonder how far away they really were. My head started spinning faster than the planet we live on. So I began with the nearest, our sun. Eventually I published a paper, which was well received. We academics, of course, have to write in Latin, so I called it *Nova Methodus distantiam solis a terra determinandi*, which, to you and me, means a How Far Away is the Sun from the Earth. I had to laugh. Write anything in Latin and it will look and sound intelligent.

Did I say my head was spinning? That made me think, too. Well, it was either that or wander round the castle and the cathedral a few more times. So I wrote another paper, called *De observationibus pro figura telluris determinanda*. If you think that sounds preposterous, this time it's even worse in English

– Observations on Determining the Shape of the Earth. I ask you, how could anyone take me seriously after that? But they did and, get this, I won even more respect simply by going to Lappland and walking round up there. I didn't find Father Christmas, but I did see a lot of reindeer.

Mind you, it was bloody cold in Lappland, so I started thinking about whether it was colder up there than down here. You know what I did then, don't you? That's right, I published yet another paper, calling it (I'll spare you the Latin this time) Observations of Two Persistent Degrees on a Thermometer.

Did you know that the boiling point of water depends on where you are, or, more specifically, on the atmospheric pressure where you are. Whereas the freezing point of water is the same all over the planet? That's fascinating isn't it? No? Well up here in Uppsala watching the geese fly overhead passes as entertainment, and freezing buckets of water is a lot more interesting than that.

So I ask you again, what would you have done?

2☆11. WRITER'S BLOCK

Instructions: When you are ready, click on the start button, read the prompts (this week in the form of questions), choose any that inspire you, then write your story. You have 90 minutes.

Click!

That was a mistake, totally not ready. I'll put the kettle on. Have a cup of tea. Or two. Feels like I've been buttonholed into making a speech on the spot, press-ganged abruptly into some service I don't support, can't sustain. Ninety minutes of this. A quick look at the prompts, though, while the first cup is brewing. Might find something I can focus on.

How do thunderstorms form?

That's an interesting question. In "What Every Schoolboy Knows," Gregory Bateson told a good story. What was it? Something about him placing an empty conch shell on the table in front of his class and asking, "how do I know that this was once part of a living being." Ha ha, that stumped them, or so he thought until some bright spark at the back put his hand up and, on being pointed at (politely, not by way of a well-aimed piece of chalk), piped up with, "because it's a spiral."

Spirals, you see, are only formed by organic beings. Look at a shell next time you're on a beach. That clever chap thought he had won the day, but Bateson moved the focus on to storms, because they're spirals too, aren't they? The rest of that discussion centred on whether storms were alive. I like to think they are.

How does a kite fly?

Well mine never did, no matter how hard I threw the damn things up in the air or how fast I ran. Charlie Brown would have felt like a world champion kite flyer up against me. We built one once, my brothers and I, back in the days when box kites were popular. It was a striking orange, striking as in how many times it hit me on the head. These heavier-than-air structures were supposed to fly well enough to carry storm-measuring equipment? Ha, those storms must have known a thing or two, with or without spirals.

How does Fushigi work?

Don't even go there. If I knew that back then I'd have tied a few of these balls to my kite.

How do I get a passport?

Oh heck, that reminds me that mine is running out. It's been so long since I replaced it last that we've now had umpteen new laws passed concerning identity and nationality, so I'm not even sure if I qualify any more. The clerk might read my application and tell me to go fly a kite.

How do you make jello shots?

Probably with the same mix of vodka and partially hydrolyzed collagen that everyone else uses. I bet they haven't used my idea of testing the strength and consistency by bouncing them from a great height. But then, I haven't used that idea yet either, because I can't get my kite off the ground, let alone up to a great height.

How does the digestive system work?

A lot faster after a significant consumption of jello shots, I can tell you.

How do I get my passport?

Oh I see, the previous question was how do I get "a" passport. In that case the previous answer should have been to borrow my father's because I know where he keeps it. Might have a little trouble with the photo, because he has a moustache and I don't, but we can do something about that.

How do birds mate?

Swifts mate in the air, which is quite some feat, especially with all these intelligent storms and stupid kites flying around.

How does the World Cup work?

It depends which world cup you're talking about. I like that old saying that rugby is a game for barbarians played by gentlemen whereas football is a game for gentlemen played by barbarians. Once you've sorted that out in your mind, you pretty much have the answer.

How do you get a UTI?

Gosh, blush! I think this might be a typo and that the word

here should be "ute." Mind you, I know someone who caught a UTI in a ute once. Something to do with jello shots.

Where is my refund?

My new cell phone is at the bottom of a sink-full of washing up because in the last ten minutes it has rung five times and put me way off my stride. I haven't yet learned how to use it and that seemed to be the only way to silence it. Unfortunately, as it wasn't an accident, I won't be getting a refund.

Where is my cell phone?

Oh, déjà vu.

Where is my mind?

That's what I always ask myself after a weird déjà vu experience. Have I skipped back in time or have I walked across one of those Einstein-Rosen bridges, like in that film with Denzel Washington and Val Kilmer, what was it called, hmmm, oh yes, Déjà Vu.

Where is my Mind lyrics

Another tease: why would I want to get my feet in the air and my head on the ground while trying to spin around? The last time that happened was when I threw my Fushigi kite up into the middle of a thunderstorm and the string got caught around my ankles.

Where is my Refund PA?

I used to ask my father that – every year!

Where is my mind IP?

With my mind still spinning after that Fushigi kite thunderstorm experiment, I went back to my childhood (over an Einstein-Rosen bridge) and found that bright spark at the back of Bateson's class. He was such a smart arse that I decked him there and then. I mean, double-barrelled name and all.

Where is my Mind Tab?

Right now it is highly focused on what is in front of me: three cold cups of tea, four empty shot glasses and an ashtray full of half-smoked tabs. Later on, when it's dusk, I dare say it will be at the bottom of the garden with the rest of the Pixies.

Where is my liver?

While I'm sitting here trying to concentrate, the concentration of jello and vodka in my liver means that it is sitting in an ambulance on the way to ER.

Where is my order?

I only have a vague sense of my order at the moment, but I think I asked for another four shots at least an hour ago. But that might just be a feeling of déjà vu.

Where is my droid?

There is no point in trying to ring my cell phone, given where it is.

What happened to House's leg?

One bright sunny day, a few years back through the Einstein-Rosen bridge, I was having this really great game of golf when one of my shots went astray. I shouted "fore" but the group up ahead obviously didn't hear me. Later, when my liver reached hospital, they said the doctor had had an accident on his round (of golf) and was feeling indisposed.

OK, I think I'm ready to write now. Damn! The timer says I've only got five minutes left. Oh well, there's always next week. Where's that order?

2☆12. WORD MASSAGE

Contraindications completed, release forms signed, the body lay on the table, face down, naked but for a small white towel across the buttocks. He dipped his hands in the bowl of warm oil and leaned from the hip, poised. Skin touched skin and that familiar frisson of excitement trembled in his stomach and straightened his spine.

"Effortless effleurage, effortless effleurage," he repeated, silently, over and over as his practised palms moved over and over, stroking the back, relaxing in rhythm.

"Powerful petrissage, powerful petrissage," he intoned as he increased the speed, kneading and rolling, frictions with fingers and thumbs.

"Tempestuous tapotement, tempestuous tapotement," beating and pounding and cupping and hacking.

"Vivacious vibrations, vivacious vibrations," trembling his knuckles on nodes and nerves.

"Meticulous massage, meritorious massage," making the movements, melodious movements, as a song in his mind.

2☆13. THE SUPPURATION OF INDEPENDANT SEPERATION

Ah, this one looks likely, a good face with strong cheekbones. But can she spell?

"My friends say I am fun to be with, recently seperated…."

Bugger, fallen at the first fence. What about Carol underneath?

"I am an independant woman…."

And will remain so forever as far as I'm concerned. Half a brain is not much to ask for, is it? Now Fiona looks as if she might tick that box, and a few others.

"I'm told I am independent minded (so far so good) *and in any relationship I will insist on keeping my own accomodation …."*

Damn! Can't disagree with you on that, Fiona, how about a hut at the North Pole? You could *corespond* from there. Down the list we go to, aha! A medic, could be promising.

"As an acupuncture practitioner, I'm looking for a man who is happy in his own skin (well, a sense of humor at least) *but I would consider it my perogative to…."*

No no, consider it a *privelege!* After all, who am I to counter the desires of such a high-minded achiever? I think I'm wasting my time here, but we will persevere.

"Liasson...."

Not with me.

"Looking for a comitment...."

Keep looking.

"Embarassment...."

And so you should be.

Oh, what's this?

"I am a recently separated independent woman with my own accommodation, seeking a liaison with a professional man in which we can develop a mutual commitment without embarrassment."

She's the one. Photograph's not very clear, so I'll just open it up in a larger format.

What the fuck? Gabrielle!

Good grief, what's the world coming to when a man's wife goes on a dating site behind his back? And why on earth would she want to do that?

2☆14. FOR THEO, REX AND PATRICIA

The bright red alarm clock with brass bells burst into life, ringing and rattling around so frantically on its spindly feet that it fell off the mahogany top of the bedside cabinet and struggled like an agitated turtle on its back on the shag pile carpet.

William Arthur Barron swung a pyjama'd leg out from under all four blankets and aimed a gentlemanly but effective kick at the still-complaining chronometer and sent it scooting grumpily under the tallboy where its gritty belligerence ended abruptly against the skirting board.

"That's enough of that," he said out loud, without realising it. "It's my last day today, so I won't be needing your services anymore."

Indeed, William Arthur Barron spoke most of his thoughts aloud, often unaware that he was doing so, and this had been a peculiar characteristic of his since childhood when his mother discovered him adapting his prayers in church.

Dominus vobiscum, *it comes spirited too!*

He was the same at Nautical Training School, where he learned about the existence of *Theo, Rex and Patricia*, his three invisible benefactors whom, he suspected, and verbalised, "probably couldn't give a toss" whether he was successful or not. But successes he had by the shipload, literally, because he started his midshipman posting after matriculating and, after bluffing his way through his early years, gained his first command on his twenty-fifth birthday, 1ˢᵗ April, 1908. Not that you'd ever call him a fool, but the day he came into the world may explain the vocal idiosyncrasy that, had events gone a different way, could have landed him in serious trouble. As it was, speaking out against the Kaiser, albeit unconsciously, put him in good favour with his seniors in the service and promotion was rapid until war eventually broke out and William's ship took a torpedo hit as it steamed past the Scillies en route to the North Atlantic.

Some superstitious sailors might say that this was bad luck, but for William it was good fortune, because that's when he came to inhabit the building that had served him as a home ever since. First as a hospital inpatient and then, having expressed his thoughts on education as lucidly as any man before him, as a teacher of physics for, after the nurses and doctors left, the edifice returned to its former occupation as a naval school. It is true, perhaps, that his appointment as physics master may have been helped along a little by the location of the science department in the former mortuary and the consequent reluctance of demobbed alternatives to, as William put it, "share space with the bloody ghosts." But whether it was that, or William's habit of spontaneously challenging every theorem since the Sumerians first made marks in clay, he soon found that his rising popularity matched his pupils' ability to pass examinations. The words that flowed out of his mouth were jaw-droppingly outrageous, but they seemed to engender his student's with a down-to-earth confidence and by 1924 he was headmaster. In that post he excelled until today, his sixty-fifth birthday.

"Don't tell me you're going to kick me out into the street after all my years of loyal service to this esteemed institution." Most retirees would have planned ahead, but William found it too easy to speak his mind, and preferred to do so, even when he didn't know what he was going to say until he said it. Faced with this challenge from their most famous talent, the Board agreed that he should stay in an Emeritus post for as long as he saw fit. And see fit he did.

Pulling his trousers on over his suspended socks, as a gentleman always does, William reflected on thirty years of repeating "you must try harder, or you'll feel the back of my hand." Twisting his fingers around new studs to attach the starched collar to his freshly laundered shirt, which was itself decorated with a freshly-pinned CBE, William knew exactly how he was going to spend the rest of his days - as an after-dinner speaker, enjoying lazy lie-ins, Blue Ribbon cuisine and fine brandy, and telling tales of his highly respectable life in the service of *Theo, Rex and Patricia.*

2☆15. DAY OF THE JACKAL

H(e): "You always say you have a bone to pick with me, so let's sit down and work this through, only we won't have the usual argument, today we'll try Gestalt."

S(he): "Gestalt? How do you mean?"

H: "We'll adopt other personalities and look at ourselves through their eyes."

S: "Other personalities? Like the guy who delivers the pizzas?"

H: "No, nothing so simple, we'll stretch ourselves. You will be me, only not me as I am, but me as an animal. You choose which animal, but make it one that you think fits my character."

S: "Like a snake in the grass?"

H: "If you want, but remember you are going to tell my story for me, from the animal's viewpoint."

S: "Well in that case, I think you'll be a jackal."

H: "Sounds challenging. As for you, you're going to be a magpie."

S: "I don't understand why, but I will try anything once,

especially if there's a chance that you might finally see things from my side."

H: "And you likewise. But let's put a time limit on this, say, an hour tops."

S: "Suits me. How do we start?"

H: "We get into character. I'm going to slip my jacket down over my shoulders so the sleeves flap out over my hands, like so, and I'll crouch down and waggle my tail feathers around, to see how it feels."

S: "Give me a minute, I'll pull a leg off the chicken we had yesterday and gnaw on it, on all fours. Then growl a bit, and sniff just like you do when you're warming up for an argument."

H: "OK, are we ready? Let's go."

S: (jackal) "Not a lot of meat on this scrawny bone, one of your cheap buys on the way home from work yesterday. You're always looking to save money."

H: "Now now, you're supposed to be *me* as a jackal, not you."

S: "Oh, I get it. Let me try again."

S: (jackal) "Yum yum, what a delicious bone, and I only paid a few dollars for the whole chicken. Such value! There must be, what, almost a mouthful here."

H: (magpie) "Flap, flap, flap, flap. Squawk."

S: (jackal) "Growwwwwl, grunt, sniff."

H: (magpie) "I do so love shiny things, like diamonds. Will you buy me some? Glittering stones that cost a month's salary and I can keep them in my nest where they'll do nobody any good."

S: (jackal) "When I've finished this bone, I'm off to the golf course, where I can chase rabbits down holes and bring home ridiculous stories about how I almost caught the deal of my life."

H: (magpie) "I'm talking through my nose now, all squeaky and poignant, looking down it at the measly scraps you call groceries. Where's the cake? I love chocolate cream gateau, not the measly crumbs you buy me. I'm the fattest magpie on the block, but I feel starved."

S: (jackal) "Not so me, I stop off at Macdonald's without telling you. Lick my fur coat in front of that waitress bitch."

H: (magpie) "Flap, flap, flap, flap. I'm preening my feathers because the window cleaner is here. Squawk, squawk, look at me, look at me."

S: (jackal) "I'm off to the gym now, to sniff around the sweaty bodies in leotards. I can run faster than anyone on the treadmill."

H: (magpie) "I'm bored, sitting at home in the nest all day. I think I will rearrange the furniture again, not that I'd call it furniture, more like twigs and leaves stuck together with gobs of spit and trimmed with moss."

S: (jackal) "I'm bored, running off to hunt every day, knowing I'm never going to catch anything worthwhile, only the odd coney or weasel here and there. It's all pretty soul destroying."

H: (magpie) "These tatty feathers don't even moult, I'm stuck with the same old clothes year in year out. Just now and again, I'd like a new outfit, something to make me feel glamorous and colourful, like a peacock."

S: (jackal) "My fur looks like last year's door mat, scuffed and filthy. It would be great, just once in a while, to puff myself up and strut confidently, like a wolf, instead of hanging my jackal head low all the time."

H: "You know, never mind the hour, I think I'm beginning to see that bone you've been picking."

S: "And I think I'm beginning to understand why you look for little flashes of excitement, knowing you can never afford the real thing. Life's boring, isn't it?"

H: "If you're going to put it that way, yes. Even being a magpie for a few minutes has been rather exhilarating by comparison. I think I'll have another few flaps and wave my tail feathers in your face."

S: "Well, in my jackal role, you're beginning to look quite tasty, much better than this old chicken bone."

H: "Ho ho! Fancy a nibble then?"

S: "I think I do."

H: (magpie) "Flap, flap, flap, flap. Squawk, squawk, squawk."

S: (jackal) "Growwwwwl, grunt, sniff, sniff, sniff."

2☆16. LINES IN THE SAND

After Stewart died, I turned inwards, to protect myself.

There was no shortage of sympathy from those around me, but these were only the outward signs. Other people couldn't really know what was going on inside me, in my head and in my heart. But I was conscious of, and grateful for, the symbolic structure they built around me, within which I could exist alone and yet remain a member of their group.

He, Stewart, had been a tower in my life. In those early years, when we cycled together through the lanes of learning and juddered over the cobbles of hierarchical thought, he had shown me a way through. His easy way with dons and freshmen, holders and breakers of tradition, taught me a language beyond words. They all respected him, trusted him, sought out his views on liberty and justice without feeling threatened or contained.

His legacy remains underneath, a shadow cooling the heat of argument, drawing lines in the sand around the castles of self, separating but joining the ownership of ideas. We were twenty-one when I first began to understand, when I passed through that last door of youth to take my own place in the community, to acknowledge and salute but still act as my conscience pressed me without harming others.

In a year or so I will return, I will signal my acceptance of all that has passed and walk amongst them with my head up.

2☆17. EXTRA SIBLING PERCEPTION

Why they bickered all the time as kids, out there in the yard, I'll never understand, but it seemed like Maryanne could read Billy's mind and she never let up. She could suck his thoughts out of his head and spit them out of her mouth as if they were hers.

"Hey Billy, I knows it was you took Pa's corn pipe."

"Didn't!"

"Did too, and I knows where ya hid it under the porch."

"Didn't! And how'd ya know?"

"It's in that old ammo pouch ya stole from Uncle Jed."

"Didn't steal nuffink. He… he gave it to me, after I shot that coney. Said I had the best eye in these here woods and gave me his pouch, like he was real proud of me."

"So why'd he spend all day looking for it?"

"Didn't."

"Did too."

They were like two crows in a tree, cawing back and forth, tussling over territory or some rotting piece of dead meat. I still shake my head when I think of them back then. She teased him mercilessly, and yet I don't think she ever had a vicious bone in her body. Passionate, oh yes, she was passionate in everything she turned her mind to, and relentless. She's still out there campaigning for just about every cause you could think of. A champion against the evils of the world.

I remember her as a ten-year-old in her Levis, stomping out in front of that peace march, singing "Onward Christian Soldiers" with all the shout and botheration her tiny frame could muster. When she got back in the yard, her brother jabbed her in the ribs.

"Hey sis, why all the religious hymning?"

"Don't ya know Billy?"

"Sounds kinda crackpot to me."

"Just you remember, Billy, evil men have no songs, so I'm singing for the Lord."

"Pshaw!"

Twenty years later, she's caught up in something more sinister, worries me sick. And Billy's not here to give her the poke I think she needs. But him being away seems to make no difference to her. She still comes home and tells me what he's up to. How she knows is the scary bit. That airbase is top secret. You can't even drive within ten miles of it without some MP riding up on a bike and pulling you over, grilling you on what you had for breakfast and when you last heard from your grandma.

Maryanne's become real tense over the last few months, pushing her food away and crying in her sleep. What's a mother to do when she sees her loved ones in such anguish? She won't talk to me about it, that's why I wish Billy was here. Even if she didn't answer his questions either, she'd pick up on the old one-two routine out there in the yard and hit him with whatever's bugging her.

Then this morning, when I woke up and went to the bathroom to wash, I heard her out back, talking to him, only he wasn't there. She was facing the tree house, waving her arms and throwing pine cones, as if she was using him as some kind of coconut shy, knocking those burning concerns off one by one as the pines bounced off the bark.

"Hey Billy, crazy man Billy, I knows what ya doing over there."

"Boing."

"Ya think I don't, but I do. I always know'd what ya doing."

"Pyung."

"You think ya saving the world, with all that confounded tecky stuff they got ya working on."

"Thonk."

"But ya too stuck up ya own asshole to see what's happening, what's going to happen, and soon."

"Chunkkk."

"I knows what ya thinking, and right now ya knows I'm talking to ya. So listen up good."

"Dinggg."

"Since we was kids, I know'd how brainy ya was. Always know'd stuff I couldn't get ma head round, but I still know'd what ya was thinking."

"Thunkkkk."

"And I knows now that ya know stuff even they don't know. They need ya Billy, but they's lying to ya. They's telling you they's proud of you, and you're swallowing it whole, but they's lying Billy."

"Bonggg."

"They's lying to ya and unless ya come home, I can't tell ya."

"Drrrumbbb."

"Billy! You gotta come home. Right now! Or Goddammit Billy, ya gonna kill us all."

"Chack. Grark. Cawwww."

"Billy, ya stupid crazy coney, if ya can hear me, if you won't come home, then, Lord forgive me…

…you gotta kill yourself, to save the planet, before it's too late!"

2☆18. SACRED HEART

Two o'clock and she was obviously not coming. So he picked up the bread in his hands and broke it with expert fingers. Then he poured some wine out of the carafe with an ease of movement that spoke of long practice. He could almost hear the words in his head, but blocked them before they reached his mouth. "There'll be no more of that," he breathed out as a sigh, inaudible above the background music in the market square café.

Three years at ecumenical college, five more in the seminary, then twenty-two years at the bishop's bidding; a whole generation watching over others as they were born, grew up and married and died in the faith. Now what did he have to show for it? He inadvertently reached into his pocket to feel his collar, his former badge of office, now held close at hand for reassurance in this new direction.

She had arrived in his church on his forty-fifth birthday, sitting demurely in the front pew with her face shining up at him as if angels had blessed her and sent her to him, a messenger to shore up his weakening faith. He stuttered a little in his sermon that day. He coughed when he gave her communion. The hand she shook on leaving was shaking and damp. There was no question about Satan getting behind him when he asked her to meet him the following Sunday in the sacristy.

He had fallen at the first, failed before the test had begun, lost before he even knew where he was. That was three years ago today, and what had he done in that time? True, he had prayed, but while his words spoke of vocation and a stout heart, his thoughts wished otherwise. True, also, that he had sought guidance with his mouth, but his ears remained deaf to any answer that excluded her from his life.

In his childhood he had known he was capable of the most powerful and enduring love. It had seemed natural, back then, to feel that love during Mass, kneeling beside his mother and sister. He had never questioned himself beyond their own commitment. He had felt his passion subsumed within that of the small village community. He had felt their pride when he announced his decision.

It was so long ago that he had forgotten the warmth of nurturing, the steady absorption of his nature into the extended family of the church. There, he had felt safe to allow his emotions to blossom into agape, an unselfish love of all beings.

But on that day when she appeared, three years ago, he had turned inwards, away from the wider world. He became, in an instant, aware of his own self. He felt different, alive in a way he had never felt before. The doubts that had arisen since the death of his mother took hold and strengthened. He heard his thoughts. He listened to his pulse beating and wondered whether his heart could ever be sacred again.

He was not a weak man. He had continued to perform his duties with dedication even under this new threat. His parishioners loved him as their guide; but he knew he had lost his map. North was now south and south was west and he could no longer look to the east with the same devotion because now he knew a different love. It overwhelmed him.

He took the only course of action he felt was open to him. He tried to ignore her. He put her to the back of his mind but there she was, every Sunday, within a few feet of him. She joined the choir. She volunteered for every church activity. She turned up on the parish council. Wherever he looked, she was there.

"If there is a God," he prayed, "then take her from me or give her to me forever."

Then, only a week ago, he had an epiphany. The words came through with a strength that allowed no denial. "Love was here first." He didn't fully understand, but he knew that his love for God was no different to his love for her. He went to see the bishop.

In the café, he took his hand out of his left pocket and reached, with the other hand, into his right pocket and felt the small case that held the ring. Was this what he had to show for thirty years? Now that she wasn't coming? He had another sip of the wine, another morsel of the bread, and stood up to leave, just as she arrived, running through the doorway, bumping into the waitress.

"Sorry I'm late," she half-choked, catching her breath, her chest heaving, her face glowing.

2☆19. THE MARLOWE LOVE KIT

Koz opened the box with a bomber's touch, gingerly, as if the contents would spill out and break on the concrete floor of the disused warehouse. Bam looked over Koz's shoulder, a woollen beany pulled down low over his eyebrows, for protection, just in case. Four wild eyes squinted under the lid, visually sniffing with feral awareness, then opened in shock to stare at the book inside.

"Wazzat manbo!?" Koz's cry was half question, half attack, a mix of approach that had kept him alive.

"Issa book. Like back wembo man, in dez olun daze." Bam lifted a forefinger and pressed down on the cover, rolling the pad from left to right, testing, confirming, while subconsciously making his mark, leaving his dab. But Koz knocked his hand away.

"Liv dat lon man. U brake de majik." He lifted the book out of the box and brushed it with his sleeve, wiping away Bam's trespass. He turned it over, weighed it in his hand, brought it up to his nose and inhaled. All the while, his eyes moved up, down and sideways, looking for thoughts that didn't come. He picked up the box and shook it, but there was nothing else. No phials, no powders, no needles, no pipes. It had to be magic. But doubts flicked the switches in Koz's mind and he stared darkly out of the open doors, towards the river.

"Dat ol coney, he dun me. Dissa no luv kit. How I mak

dreems wit dis?" He tossed the book down in the dirt and walked out, reaching behind his back to grasp the hilt of his knife.

"I fine U ol man, der be a rekoning."

Bam squatted down to retrieve the book, and settled on his knees and heels. He could just about remember, but without any detail. He dug deeper and touched a memory of feelings, of awe and fascination. He stroked the leather spine. It had a certain beauty, a texture that pulled him out of the present. With a kind of reverence, he tilted the binding and let the pages fall open.

With his craggy fingertip, he followed the contours of the print, up the hills and down the valleys, moving his lips, making the mouth shapes as he recalled the mountains of the past.

Cum liv wit me and be my Luv,
    An we will tak our plezzurs Bruv.

It would be a struggle, but Koz would know; Koz would remember, eventually.

2☆20. FAIRY TALE

"That's my shoe."

"Tisn't."

"Of course it is, look, I've only got one on."

"Yours is brown, this one's black."

"Makes no odds, I need another and I saw it first."

"Didn't."

"Did too. What you want with it anyway?"

"It's magic."

"Magic baloney."

"Sure it's magic. I heard something like it once. There was this old woman and she lived in a shoe."

"How can you live in a shoe?"

"I told you, it's magic. I bet if I rub it, you know, like Alldin and his lamp, it'll turn into a house that I can live in."

"You mean Aladdin? And his lamp didn't turn into a house, there was a genie living in it."

"Well there you go then, if the genie was living in the lamp, it must have been his house."

"That's just a stupid fairy tale. It don't mean nothing. It's not real, but that shoe's real enough, and I need it for my other foot."

"You're not having it. This old woman that I heard about, she had a lot of children, and that's what I want. I'm going to live in a house and have lots of kids. So this magic shoe is what I need."

"You want kids? We could have kids, you and me."

"I want a house."

"I know where there's an empty log cabin in the woods. You give me that shoe and I'll show you."

"A dirty smelly old log cabin?"

"We could clean it up. We could have a cabbage patch, to get all the kids, and I could chop firewood to sell. You could sew some curtains. It'd be neat."

"Curtains?"

"Yeah."

"Hmmm, I guess we could."

"So come on, give me the shoe."

"How do you know it'll even fit you?"

"Let me try it on, then, if it does fit, you'll know I'm the one for you."

"What, like that story about Cinderellia?"

"Yeah, I'll be your prince."

"OK then, but if it doesn't fit, I'm having it back."

2☆21. NERIDA'S YOUTH

I only paint dreams. The colours are more vivid than in real life, which carries the grays of sadness and despair. That's why I use acrylics. You can't get the same effect with watercolours, because, like life's experiences, they fade as your brush is touching the paper.

The tones I try to reach are like the air we breathe, changing from in to out, from yin to yang, moving across the scene like ghosts, their dresses swirling in the unseen wind.

Yesterday I was an antelope, today a duck, and tomorrow I will be a pack of playing cards, incising the moment, stretching it onto canvas, leaving an indelible memory that I can recall in my sleep, because I only paint dreams.

2☆22. RAIN MAN

He paused to remove his white coat and hang it carefully on the hook behind the door. I closed my eyes and pictured him doing this at home, changing from psychiatrist to family man in one easy movement. In this situation, however, the clothes did not maketh the man.

"OK Adam," he said pulling the chair out from underneath the plain wooden table, "what we want to do today is to try out a kind of sophisticated Rorschach test, to show you pairs of words or pictures that might stimulate the two halves of your brain."

I moved my focus to the backs of my eyelids and saw the gentle billowing of the clouds high up above the mountain ridge to the west.

"Here's the first." I heard him lean over to slide a piece of paper across the table, the high-pitched scrape of his chair echoing the cry of the eagle in my other world.

"Redact – Detract. Adam, are you looking at this?"

They're clever, I'll give them that. But they would not have found the notebook if it hadn't been for the accident. It's not even mine, but they'll be looking for a reason to redact the content and detract from its meaning. I can tell what's coming next.

"How about this one Adam? Can you hear me? Denial – Puerile?"

Puerile? There's no denial that it's childish, but puer takes me back to when I was a boy, out on the plains. My family were with them, but not of them. White people living as native Americans, touching the depths of our very existence. They named me. My potential had been understood the moment I was born. I had the gift and my inner nature was nurtured with every breath I took. When the time came to leave the world of childhood behind, I wandered for months with the shaman's spirit, taking with me my father's passion and my mother's love, absorbing the folklore of the forefathers, the whispers of the wild.

I returned to be embraced. The shaman stood erect in the centre of the circle and held his arms to the sky. He was the judge, the one who could see beyond the dust of the days, the one with the wisdom of a hundred owls who could guide his people out of the drought. When I had left with him I was just a boy, childish in my thoughts, but when I returned he called to the spirits to welcome me as a man. I was now part of them, an individual without separation, one who could leave this earth, touch the cosmos, and return to spread the universal love throughout the tribe.

The circle began to move, first clockwise then counter, stamping and chanting.

"This sacred earth beneath our feet, with every step we take. Unite my people, be one, be one."

They named me Rain Man, for such was my gift.

"The earth is our mother, we must take care of her. Unite my people, be one, be one."

"Come on now Adam. Try these two, Collude – Delude."

Like Freud and his slips, he was talking more about himself than me. His world rather than mine. Collusion is safety, but comes at the price of delusion. If he agrees with all around him then he speaks the truth. He delights in the finite, whereas I take my joy in the infinite, the One that is open to all but denied through fear.

Fear is a powerful but false union. When I was sent to plant the seeds in the world of organisations, and to water them, it was fear that blocked. Oh yes, I was successful, and they were grateful for the growth I brought. They didn't understand my skills or how I worked, but they called me "Rain Maker." It allowed them to separate me without actually letting me slip outside their world. It was their way of integrating me into their group. It was only a short step to ask the question, *why* "Rain Maker" but it was a question nobody asked because that would have taken me outside of their world.

"Adam, open your eyes, look at this picture of Two Boots."

I don't need to open my eyes to see his dance, heavy on the one hand, but ever so light on the other, as if on ice, treading delicately over my diagnosis lest he slip and lose control. He'll be wanting to make a breakthrough and publish his paper; a new syndrome? Already my autism quotient has been misunderstood, but it's important for his other clients, parents who bring their children to him but who will not accept the strangeness that makes them strangers in their own families. Strangely, the parents are proud, "my son has

Aspergers." If only they knew. It will only be a matter of time until Aspergers is merged with Tourettes to give another acceptable face of rebellion. Ha! That would be good. We could call it Aspettes and then I could say to the doctors, "I'm an autistic savant, *now fuck off!*"

I came close to bridging the gap. When that young reporter came to ask me whether I had special powers. He talked in obscure sentences that hinted without saying. He talked in roundabout terms about Russian experiments with ESP and precognition, astral planing, and meditative insight. But he had no inner patience himself and I could see he was only after a story, to be told then filed on his CV. When he left, he pulled his coat tightly around him, opened his umbrella, and strode out to catch a cab, muttering under his breath that "it never rains but it pours." He left his notebook on the table and I ran after him, but he didn't hear me.

It was the rain that caused the accident. An old Plymouth convertible was caught in the cloudburst and the driver wiped his eyes at the crucial moment. His career ended mine as he collided with the hot dog stand I was passing. Nothing seriously wrong with me physically, but they say that I have extensive psychological damage. They couldn't fix it, but they found the notebook and, at long last, started to ask those difficult questions that will absolve them from their concerns.

So now I'm here inside an institution being asked more questions that seek desperately to place me somewhere inside their society. Outside, in the corridors, I hear my former colleagues steadily distancing themselves from me, changing Rain Maker into Rain Man.

Only this time it's *their* Rain Man, not my Rain Man.

☆☆☆☆☆☆☆☆☆☆☆☆☆☆☆☆☆☆☆☆☆

THE STORIES - VOL.3

☆☆☆☆☆☆☆☆☆☆☆☆☆☆☆☆☆☆☆☆☆

3☆1. PHARMAVERBUM MEDISEMANTICS

My five-year-old grandson Ben tore into the room, his superhero cape flying high behind his outstretched arms, saw me sitting comfortably in my favourite armchair, and sprang. His scrunched up knees landed painfully on my chest, expelling the air from my lungs in an old man's gasp. Unfazed, he turned his angelically innocent face towards mine and tugged on my beard.

"Tell us a story Grandpa."

"Mmmurggle pphhhffffff," was all I could manage.

"Go on, go on, go on, tell us a story."

"Well I dunno," I winced, his sandalled foot stretching downwards into my groin.

He grabbed my ears, pushed his snotty nose into mine, and giggled.

"What's so darn funny littl'un?" I gurgled through his dribble.

"I just done a botty burp." More sniggering.

Lifting him up to relieve the pressure on my gonads, I sighed then laughed.

"OK then, what's it to be? A fairy tale?"

"No, no, no, Grandpa. You know, one of yours."

I did know. In my time I've travelled the world and have been guilty of telling a few of my own fairy tales. But they had gone down well with my son, who was thrilled to hear about sailing boats and faraway cities, and now Ben was following in the anecdotal footsteps.

"Are you sitting comfortably then?" Because this is how all stories begin.

He shook his head and, struggling to free his cape from under his bottom, slipped and fell backwards, hitting his head on the carpet with a loud thump. Laughter turned abruptly to a loud siren of wails, staccatoed with gulps like bubbly hiccups. His mother was instantly by his side, expecting the worse. She picked him up with oven-gloved hands and jiggled him on her shoulder but he would not be soothed.

"It's OK Anne, he's fine, just a tiny bump, leave him with me and I'll make it all better with a story."

She gave me a look that suggested she'd heard enough of those already, but she thought better of it, plonked him back on my lap and went into the kitchen, both ears pinned to the ether.

"Does it hurt?" I asked him quietly, "Should I rub it better?" I lifted my hand towards his head but he pushed it away.

"That doesn't work," he simpered, "it never works. I want a aspring."

"A what?" I was horrified. "An aspirin? Why would you want one of those?"

"To make the hurt go away. Mummy takes them all the time. I've seen her."

"Does she now? Well I don't think you should be popping pills at your age." My eyes narrowed and I met his lowbrowed stare. "I tell you what, we'll use Pharmaverbum Medisemantics, that'll get you better in no time."

His back arched and his eyes opened wide. His gob was clearly smacked.

"The farmers bum middle sandwiches?"

"Ha ha, no. I said we'll use Pharmaverbum Medisemantics."

"Farmer, farm, ffff...." His voice slowed to a crawl and then parked just behind his teeth, his lips pressed hard together.

"Did I ever tell you about the time I was walking in the mountains and fell down a ravine?"

He shook his head again. He was obviously intrigued and had stopped whimpering.

"Well, now, when was it. Must have been forty years ago, I'd stopped for some lunch and went off to find some kindling for the fire. There were hardly any trees, but I came across a dead bush hanging over the edge of a dried up river valley. You know what comes next, don't you? I leaned out to break off a branch and missed my footing. Silly old fool. I bumped and tumbled down a hundred feet of scree before landing heavily with my right leg underneath me. Boy that hurt."

Ben slapped my chest with both palms. "How much Grandpa? How much did it hurt? Was it like when I fell off the gate yesterday?"

"Oh no, far worse than that."

"Was it like when I burned my hand on the kettle?"

"Worse than that, but you're getting closer."

"Did it hurt as much as my head hurts now?"

"You know, I think you've got it, my leg hurt as much as your head does. So what was I going to do? I didn't have an aspirin. Well I did, but that was in my backpack up the top of the ravine."

"You should have called Daddy."

"Oh I would have, except your Daddy wasn't born then, and this was long ago, way before we had mobile phones or anything like that, so when I hit the bottom I was on my own with no way of telling anyone where I was. No phone, no aspirin, and my leg hurting like your head. Ah, I was in a sorry state."

"Couldn't you rub it better?"

"I tried, Ben, I tried. But as you said, that doesn't always work."

"So what did you do?"

"That's what I am trying to tell you, I used Pharmaverbum Medisemantics. Now before you ask again, this is an archaic but powerful language that uses words to blow away the pain."

"Words? Like a magic spell?"

"Exactly that. You're getting my drift now. Yes, some words can be stronger than medicine, but they have to be the right words."

"Which words?"

"I'm getting to that. But we have to speak quietly now, because these words are so strong that we wouldn't want your mother to hear them and get frightened. They're only to be used in extreme circumstances and then only by people in pain."

"You're not in pain Grandpa."

"Oh, that's right. Tell you what, pinch me somewhere, then that will give me just enough pain so I can whisper them, then you can repeat them. Don't worry if you can't say them exactly, the words will know what you're trying to do."

OUCH!" The little blighter had squeezed my nose with all his might and, I don't mind saying, it really hurt.

"I really need to say one now. Analgesiverpa. That's the first one, now you say it."

"Ann all cheesy fur pa."

"Brilliant! How do you feel?"

He looked sideways.

"OK, try another one. Paracetamentulice."

"Parrots eat a mantelpiece."

"Oh you're getting good at this. One final one, the strongest. Morphutuo."

"More future oh."

"That's it. Now you're cured."

He blinked, waggled his eyes from side to side, then giggled again.

"You're right Grandpa, it doesn't hurt any more."

"I told you so, now off you go and wash your hands, dinner is almost ready."

He slid off my lap like a rabbit and shot up the stairs, his superhero cape flying high behind his outstretched arms.

3☆2. OUR LADY OF ASSUMPTIONS

I lived in a bubble. Not my bubble: one of their bubbles.

What they used for soap I'll never know, but it was practically impenetrable. Not all that soft, either, as bouncing around inside was a bruising experience. That said, their argument was that bruising was not life-threatening. That's why they put us in the bubbles in the first place, to protect us from harm, but only one of us per bubble, so I lived in my own bubble, on my own.

Until I finally managed to burst the membrane, and see the world for what it really is, I simply didn't, couldn't, know anything for certain. Life was a daily series of assumptions, every one built on the last, like a pyramid of beliefs, except they're all of one hue, the colour of the soap. There's no variation. Now that I've escaped my bubble, I know that mine was blue, but looking around me I can see that there are many different colours, though it seems that a high proportion in my country are blue.

Now and again I bump into somebody else who's lost their bubble and we sit and chat and watch the world bumbling along with nothing more than a bruising experience, happy and safe within their assumptions.

3☆3. TALK AND CHEESE

Colin couldn't think what to say to Sabrina.

He felt enormously proud that she'd agreed to go to the prom with him, but he didn't understand why. She was easily the brightest girl in the class and hoped to become a teacher herself. He, a self-confessed geek, had peculiar interests, the most passionate of which was making cheese.

Sabrina pursed her dark mauve lips around the diet cola straw and blew. The liquid bubbled.

He babbled, launching into unnecessary froth.

"The cheese mite is a fraction of a millimetre long, invisible to the naked eye, but if you see a brownish dust on the rind of a piece of cheese, you know it's infested with mites. It's their legs and antennae that are brown."

Sabrina sucked and the cola gurgled in the lumps of ice at the bottom of the cup.

He gargled, the words getting stuck like lumps in the back of his throat.

"They are also quite partial to cured meats, and flour, but cheese is their particular favourite. If you're cheese is infested, they're pretty difficult to get rid of. You can brush them off the cheese, but you have to wipe all your surfaces and containers down all the time."

Sabrina slowly drew the straw out of the plastic lid, screeching the quartered lips of the cross-cut hole.

His voice squeaked, with heightened tension.

"Some cheese makers use mites to help fermentation, in, say, Spinnenkaese and Milbenkaese. They think it gives them added flavour, sweet and minty. You eat the mites along with the cheese."

The straw dribbled on the melamine table, forming meniscus tuffets of brown liquid that Sabrina squashed with her finger into flat spiders.

He dribbled, struggling like a helpless fly in the web of her gaze.

"Personally, I wouldn't touch any of that stuff. I think the only thing more disgusting than a cheese mite is their Latin name, Tyrophagus Putrescentiae, which sounds like it means that they eat shit."

He scrabbled, looking for threads that might stick.

"They cause all kinds of skin and respiratory allergies, dermatitis, grocer's itch and asthma. They're real mean boogers."

Sabrina prized the top off the cup and inverted it on the table, hearing the ice crackle as it spluttered on the formica.

His voice cracked, then stuttered.

"D d d do you, er, I mean, w w w would you like to, ummmm?"

Sabrina's black lashes whipped open wide and her cold green eyes slapped Colin's flushed cheeks.

"What?" she asked.

He gulped.

"Um. Er. I was just wondering. Would you like to… dance?"

Sabrina flipped over the empty cup, sending the ice dancing across the floor, and held it out to Colin.

"I'd like another cola."

3☆4. HEAD HUNTER

Selling. He should have thought of it years ago instead of wasting a decade in academia.

True, he had the brains for a PhD, a good head on his shoulders, as his father used to say. But that was really hard work whereas selling was, as they said in the business, a piece of piss. Give people what they want, he chuckled to himself, and they'll go out and do the work for you, telling all and sundry how you're the best thing since sliced bread. Behind the laugh was a nod, because he also understood that, although people might tell you that they want this or that, what they *really* want is an entirely different matter. Finding it was his particular skill.

The phone rang and a voice said: "I'm interested in what you have. I'd like to…" and click, the line went dead. He waited for a minute in case it rang again, then dialled number recall, scribbling it down with a pencil. When he returned the call, it was an answerphone. No matter, he would chase later that day and every day until he got through to the man, his new prospect. He spoke out loud, an affirmation, "whatever he wants, I've got it."

It took a month of persistent trying but, when he finally heard that voice again, it said: "Just as I thought, you have the intelligence, and the tenacity to make the best use of it. I am definitely interested in what you have to offer." So an appointment was made for that very afternoon.

The demonstration he laid on was perfect. Doubly tested, the right backdrop and lighting, the most seductive soft leather chair, a secretary primed to bring strong coffee and sugar-high fudge on his signal. It was all a blind, of course, a stratagem on which to base his questions aimed at the real purpose of the meeting. Effectiveness and efficiency, savings and growth, were all bollocks. What people wanted was always personal.

The old man entered wearing an old-fashioned but impeccably tailored black suit. In one hand he held a silver-topped cane. In the other, he carried a large leather Gladstone, which he set down on the coffee table. Ignoring the seat proffered, he walked slowly over to the window and looked down into the carefully tended gardens. He's good, thought the younger man, he's settling himself before getting down to business. He allowed several minutes to pass before opening his own pitch, on a personal note.

"I love gardens, they create such a sense of peace."

"Indeed they do," replied the old man, "especially when they are properly pruned." His voice was the same as that on the phone, but with an added edge. He moved away from the window and into the room as he turned the question around, "Would you not agree?"

"Pruned? Why of course, but you have to choose the right time for each plant."

We've struck an accord here, the younger man thought, and smiled, but where's he going with the pruning? Is he looking to cut staff and is feeling a little guilty? But he doesn't look it, there's a determination about him that is rarely seen.

"Are you aware of the true cost of what I'm after?" said the old man. A common question, but posed in a strange way. A good opportunity to fish.

"Well that depends on what you *are* after. Would you like to give me a head's up here?"

"You're very perceptive. I'm not in the slightest bit interested in your product; what I want is a piece of you."

The younger man didn't flinch. He'd learned his trade. But *that* was it, he thought. The old man is a head hunter, he's here to recruit me. It will be another selling job, of course, but I'd be interested to know what sort of money he's talking. He nudged the conversation towards rewards and upped the growing tension.

"I'm happy to hear what you have to offer, if you're ready."

"Oh I'm ready," the old man said with a stare, "but are you? Is this the right time?"

The younger man felt a bizarre excitement. "Well there's an argument that it's never the right time, but I always say that if you want to get ahead, there's no time like the present."

"My feelings exactly." The old man opened his Gladstone and took out a large glass jar with a hinged lid and orange rubber seal. Then with a practised movement, he twisted the silver top on his cane and out slid a stainless steel blade.

"I'll take it now."

3☆5. A COMPULSORY EXPERIENCE IN SOLITUDE

When I was a child, Christmas was a time of inescapable excitement. We could feel our stomachs tightening with each day that passed, clambering out of bed, ignoring the frost on the inside of the windows and clustering around the courtier stove to open our advent calendars before dressing for school.

The long dark evenings were brightened with tinsel and sticky-taped paper chains, which we hung from candelabra to cornice like alternating rays of starlight and colour. Harry was old enough to use the stepladder, so I held the legs tightly and giggled as Dick jumped up and down to pass up the coils of loops, which Harry then dropped over our heads with feigned clumsiness and laughter.

The tree was even more fun, always a foot taller than Harry could reach with the silver star. So he'd bend it this way and that, then flick the star off again when he let go. We'd stand on the backs of the sofa and chairs to hang the lights and glass orbs, using twisted pieces of wire to hold them all in place. When finished, we'd run upstairs to ferret out the presents we'd wrapped and hidden in cupboards and under beds, to arrange them haphazardly below the bottom branches, our faces glowing with anticipation.

When I was an adult, I taught my children to approach the season with the same sense of exhilaration, the same thrill of preparation. I'd sit down with them and the pots of glue and coloured paper, dab their noses with the brush, wind tinsel into garlands for their heads, buy the tallest tree I could find, and leave all my loose change lying around as if by accident, so they could splash out a little more on gifts for the family.

Now my children are adults, they are passing on this tradition in their own homes; Thomas in New York, Richard in Dubai, and Harriet in Sydney. I see them on Facebook and talk to them on Skype, and when I do I can sense that same tornado of excitement that blew through the house in my youth. But they're all just a little too far away to reach with a human hand. So when I close the lid of my laptop, the storm passes over me and I put the kettle on for a cup of tea.

3☆6. A CLOSE SHAVE

Jeremiah Todd laid out the tools of his trade on the scrubbed wooden table beside the chair. The leather strop he had inherited from his grandfather, the newly bought razor made from the best Birmingham steel, the Staffordshire pottery mug of soapy foam and the freshly laundered Christie towels. Then there was the chair itself, built out of oak to the original design, with soft kapok padding to lull his customers halfway to sleep. But Jeremiah himself was tense. A feeling of sharp anticipation crept up his body and down his arms to make his fingers tingle. He would show them, after all those years of waiting, he would exact an appropriate revenge for the slander on his family.

Isaiah Thornhill scraped his breakfast eggshells carefully onto torn out pages of a penny dreadful and folded them into a neat package, to be disposed of on his walk into town. He had not slept. Instead, he had cleaned the diminutive tenement house from top to bottom. He knew it was a poor effort compared to Johanna's meticulous attention to the smallest detail, but it would do in the circumstances. He knew she wouldn't mind the odd stain here or there or the occasional missed cobweb. She had been so understanding.

At six o'clock that morning Isaiah had drawn a hot bath, the water almost scalding from the copper, and lain for an hour soaking away the anxiety. Ten years alone was enough and those who said that time was a great healer were offering an uninformed palliative that was ill judged and self-appeasing.

His pain had never eased and he felt now that he was drowning in the depth of his grief. So yesterday he had resolved to end it, to bring to a close the days he spent as an automaton, acting out his façade of bravado and courteous bearing in public whilst shedding wretched tears in private. But he would bring no shame on his wife or his widower status by leaving an untidy abode. He doubted she would have been that understanding.

Taking off his bathrobe in the bedroom, he dressed carefully, tugging his collar into shape, looping his tie as she used to like it, smoothing down the nape of his jacket and fastening his newly-polished buttons so that they stood proud and erect. Running his fingers through his drying hair, he checked himself in the mirror on the inside door of the mahogany wardrobe that she treasured as a keepsake from her mother. Yes, he reflected without any trace of conceit, you will meet her again looking your best. The back of his hand brushed gently against his cheek and he winced at the coarse feel of stubble. He opened the tallboy, took out his razor and laid it gently down on the dressing table. This was to be his instrument and he wondered, briefly, whether he should make it look like an accident before deciding firmly that this would make him feel like a coward. He turned the blade and scraped it against his palm. He wasn't ready yet, he had the time, he would go into town for a professional shave.

The early morning air was fresh on his skin and a snow had settled on the seats in Lincoln's Inn Fields, camouflaging them as Christmas cakes. The pond was half frozen and the trees shifted uneasily as he walked past, shaking a little under the weight of their burden, almost as if they shared his. As he came out into Serle Street, he quickened his pace, slipped on the kerb, dropped the package of eggshells and stumbled onto the road into the path of a lorry turning out of Carey Street. His brain worked at ice-cold speed, sparking thoughts he could never have imagined. Death, too soon, he wasn't ready, and he hadn't had a shave. Then, as the lorry was almost upon him, in the still-dark dawn he saw Johanna's face in the headlights.

Five minutes later, still stunned, he was sitting on the cobbles holding his head. He couldn't believe he had been so stupid. He had the precious gift of life with wholesome memories of Johanna and yet he was about to end it. This was a sign, he knew, an omen and she was telling him from beyond the grave to honour her with his life. When his insides had melted and his muscles had stopped their involuntary shaking he stood cautiously. The next step was like his first, tentative and trusting whereas that morning they had been measured and funereal. He would live; he knew it now.

Walking slowly as he reflected on his close shave with death, he mused that it would be appropriate to begin his new lease of life with a real close shave, at Jeremiah Todd's barber shop. Holding his head higher, he turned more confidently into Carey Street and then Bell Yard. As he passed Lovett's Bakery the aroma teased his mind and he resolved to buy a pie for lunch.

3☆7. ELIOT RECOLLECTS

It is so long ago now, difficult to remember, hard to recall. It's in my ether, but the words I used and why I used them, escape me now. It's over fifty years since the clarity that came of youth and purpose sharpened my pencil and my wits. And even then it took me years, and the heavy breathing histories of Harvard, Paris and Munich.

For me it had more mood than meaning. The Frenchman would tell you, his factories' hundred throats blowing smoke to the sky. Two cents of skirt and a pair of eyes, and what comes after, that might relieve the boredom. But I have never looked into a woman's soul. So I have wasted love.

The smoky thoughts that do arise out of long gone chimneys in my mind reach up and out to my nostrils now and smell of decay. This was the time of Hardy, his Century's corpse my patient on the table, and my evening spread out against the sky his cloudy canopy. All you had to do was to wake up and open your eyes to see it was a time of death.

The game has been to guess the name and where it came from, but to me it has no relevance. Whether furniture makers or bureaucratic dullards sit behind my man and lift their skirts to show their greying credentials, I neither remember nor care. What visions come are ones of childhood, adolescence, and unspeakable suffocation, the smog of overpowering perfume and the threat of powdered sex, pinned under hats and hairpieces.

I borrowed Kipling's Love Song, but I heard the words he used - alone, weary, captives, old, harsh, drudge, sorrow, tears; come back to me, Beloved, *or I die*.

But mostly the poetry that I needed to teach me the use of my own voice did not exist in English at all; it was only to be found in French. So Jules was my mood muse, Jules was my heart, my mind, my pair of eyes and my voice. With Jules beside me we brayed at our bleached and atrophied souls and cried out to the wind, 'You too, you crooked old fart!'

3☆8. TONGUE-TIED

He looked at her.

She looked at him.

He licked his lips.

She raised her eyebrows, inviting him to speak.

"I came…." But the voice died in his throat. She sat impassively, watching his face.

"I wanted. Want. Need."

He stretched his fingers, then clenched his fists, feeling the dampness in his palms.

The clock behind him ticked softly. The diplomas on the wall said he could trust her, but he wasn't so sure. She was, after all, a woman. The same sex as his wife. Former wife. Ex-wife.

"I…. *She*…."

He looked away from her eyes, down to her understated jacket, around her lap-folded hands, onto her long tie-died skirt that was so similar to the one *she* had bought from Macy's. Along with that hat. For her wedding. Her *second* wedding. The hat with the wide brim, wide enough to hide her eyes. Her thoughts. Who could have known what she was going to do?

"My…."

The hands on the unseen clock measured his painful failure to express his pain. Who could have known? How could she do this? Take away his son.

"He's not…. "

He couldn't bring himself to voice the word. *Dead*. But his shoulders dropped in defeat. His son may as well be dead, passed over into that place where he is inaccessible, as he now was, thousands of miles away. Death, at least, would bring grieving. Inward sorrow and outward condolence. Family acceptance and understanding.

"He's…."

In another place. Another country. Another world. Not his anymore.

Talk to him, they said, but how could he? His calls unanswered. His emails blocked. His letters returned.

Talk about it, they said. Go and see someone. See? See someone other than his son's face?

His mother's face hidden under that hat. Her plans hidden behind her unseen eyes.

A few short steps from the Court to the car. A few short miles to the airport.

The long hours of every day alone. But here he was. Seeing someone.

He looked at her.

She looked at him.

"I...."

3☆9. THE TASK OF THE DAY

He started it to relieve the boredom. Then it had become a habit, and now it was built into his daily routine, as natural to him as eating and sleeping.

He would work out the details over breakfast. Nothing too complicated, but it had to be challenging enough to raise his heart rate. He could achieve this without too much risk if he avoided the powerful and focused on the nonentities that he might not otherwise notice. "The pawns," he told himself, "are the soul of the game."

Yesterday, he had to make someone save him from falling flat on his face. The taxi rank outside the store proved to be the perfect place. He had chosen a woman laden up to her chin with brown paper bags, standing at an angle, facing away from the others, musing, half in and half out of her world, pondering on her problems while staying just awake enough to see him out of the corner of an eye and react on instinct.

He had adopted an air of casual indifference while singing the first line from "Oh what a beautiful morning," forcing the "ing" upwards in feigned surprise as he tucked one toe behind a heel and stumbled forwards with his hands in his pockets. "Oh my God," she'd half-shouted, dropping her bags on the sidewalk and reaching out to him with both arms. With her groceries hiding her chest, he hadn't noticed how well endowed she was. That was a bonus: such a warm and soft landing. They had picked up her shopping together and stayed chatting while cabs came and went and in the end he'd given her a lift home. These secondary effects were unplanned but, when they happened, they made the challenge all the more rewarding.

Today, he would put his fingers into someone's collar, down the back of the neck. It shouldn't be too difficult to find an excuse, but he would derive the obligatory emotional stimulus from the human contact. Another pawn, he decided, man or woman it didn't matter, but preferably in their twenties or thirties this time.

The weather was kind to him, the hot sun bringing the office workers out into the park at lunchtime to eat their bagels on the benches under the rhododendrons. He walked slowly along the path and caught sight of a spider dropping from a leaf and climbing back up its thread. "Ah," he thought, a ready-made premise, for there, directly underneath it, sat a young woman eating a bun that was far too sticky for her own good.

"Excuse me," he said softly, "but a spider has just fallen onto your collar."

The scream knocked him backwards like a blow to the head. Shrill and piercing and was it ever going to end? She was off that bench as if it had ten thousands volts through it, stamping her feet and waving her hands around her head, slapping at her neck, then fumbling with the buttons on her blouse. She had half of them undone before he was able to achieve the task of the day and reassure her that he had got the little beast and that she was insect free. A Starbucks later and she was calm enough to return to work.

He walked home with her phone number and pondered her reaction. Perhaps he should have let her continue disrobing. He might try that ruse again sometime and choose a particularly attractive prey. A real spider placed deftly and visibly on the lapel might heighten the tension and prolong the response. His cleaner wasn't due until Friday and he wondered whether he might find a suitably large bugger up behind one of the pelmets.

With creativity, this variation of the game could last him a whole week.

3☆10. MAKE YOUR BED

We stood upright in the sand, we four, in the circle that makes the square, and prayed to the God who lived in our heads. Our toes tensed and tightened through the sand, groping for grip that wasn't there. We'd lost our grasp on certainty the moment the main broke and the carrack turned keel up. Yet we stood upright now, making a new normality out of what was around us, above and below.

The day we were shipwrecked the storm abated into the most glorious sunny afternoon. What a dichotomy. A morning of wrath and tempest and then a translucent settling of warmth and wonder breathing over our battered bodies. We could find no sense in it and thereafter we were threatened with a sensual survival, surrounded by dramatic colors and inhaling intoxicants wafting from unrecognized blooms, nudging us unconsciously into a different reality.

Our world changed. Bread from fruit not wheat, and milk from coconuts not cows; water from a cataract we found not a mile from the surf but further still from our imagination. For physicality ruled us daily and our fears returned by night. Where was the God who'd left us behind on our journey to find him in a new asylum? We prayed in churches made of palms by altars of driftwood with seaweed mantles. We offered up our sacrifice of clams and fish caught fresh from the sea, hoping to feel that bond we knew as children.

But the air we breathed in our nostrils brought nonsense to

our brains and turned us inside out. That's when we walked away from old beliefs and into a new truth stretched painfully in front of our open eyes. We had to think on separate strata, build veracity on altered footings, or go mad. So we decided, we four, to let our faith evaporate and follow, instead, the path of practicality. We lived as one, a single self-supporting organism. A sole psychology held us together, kept us going. We lost our selves to each other and left our doubts in the sand to be washed away by the tide.

When they finally came, after fifteen years, they faltered on the same reef, but this time a gentle wind lifted them up and lowered them softly just inside the barrier. Only a small hole, to be repaired within a week, and they would be away again. But seven days saw no peace amongst the crew when, sailors all, they saw a sight that made them shiver, shake their heads and swear to have no part of this. It was not natural, so they said, and worked with their heads down, their eyes and ears attentive only to their ship, avoiding what they saw here as bedlam. The captain tried to speak to us, but his words stirred painful memories of something far away and we demurred.

And so they sailed and left us, we fourteen, standing upright in the sand.

3☆11. GOOSEBERRY BUSH

If you care for a gooseberry bush, it can be productive for up to twenty years.

Propagation is simple, but there are variations in technique, depending on whether your bush is feral or cultivated.

It is advisable to keep it moist when the fruit is being formed.

If you are worried about pests, then you can keep your bush in a cage.

Opinions differ about pruning, but it is generally accepted that you should trim the older growth. When you prune, aim for a goblet shape, and open up the centre of the bush.

If you husband it in this way, then it has long been held that the gooseberry bush has powerful medicinal properties, restoring health and vitality when most needed.

3☆12. FANNY HURD

Good day to you, dear Sir, or Madam, you who brave the cemetery gates to walk in here amongst the dead, treading gently on the whispering grass, respectfully. You murmur softly amongst the stones, your thoughts still full of possibilities, of questions asked of your living God about your late-lived loved ones, friends and relatives. Do answers come to you now, in imaginings, words or voices stifled by your fear of death? Or have you read them all already in a book, a good book, or a banned obscenity transcending all those born and bred boundaries we must absorb when first we're taught to read the symbols of our civil life.

If you were down here with me you would see that social mores are more like dying and less like living, for there is so, so much more than what is taught, when tautly held within those mothering arms of confidence, so confidently smothering our faces, our early facing of the world, covering our eyelids with warm words of heaven and angels and beings of light, so lightly being within our souls, touching our dreams and wishes, confiding in our hearts so young and inexperienced, the imaginary light of truth, untruthful in the end.

Like you I danced with limbs and fingers, touching lightly the air of life, lifting my own heart up to heaven to laugh and swim fully-clothed in the promised eternity of our church, moving my existential core, my centre of gravity, little by little, one yard at a time, towards nirvana. Like you, I fingered the rails, I beat the bounds, confident in the edges of reality, safe within that white picket-fenced garden, picking the daisies that flit-fluttered like birds bathing in mud, tussling for worms half-submerged.

Now here I am in limbo, fingering the daisy roots, my footfalls in a deeper mud. Am I the one you seek? Absorbing a different air, skinny-dipping half-submerged in profundity, I cannot read your thoughts or see your faces as my boundaries have changed, the limits of your lives are no longer held within belief but extend beyond the rims of reason to touch the edges of the universe. You are both bright and dark to me, angels in the truest sense, both in and out of consciousness that passes as we pass.

3☆13. A PROPER CUP

Twisting the cap off the bottle of spa water, he inverted it over the copper kettle and the gurgling sound entered his ears.

"Drown, you bastard, drown!"

All year we'd worked our **butts** off to bring the swimming team up to scratch.

****

He clicked the switch and returned the bottle to the fridge, pulling out a packet of Columbian. Keep it cold, keep it fresh. The tin foil let out a hiss as he snipped off the top.

"I'd like to snip off your balls, if you had any!"

We put in the time, every day after school, **late** into the evening.

****

The pot chinked as he set it down on the table.

"Your potted guts should be in here. If I could find them!"

Even Thompson had turned up the heat, all those **extra** lengths to reach peak fitness.

****

Four spoons, heaped, you just cannot brew this stuff too strong. Then the water, freshly boiled but not boiling.

"Poured over your "proper procedures", you unprincipled Principal!"

All those hours in the pool, coaxing and cajoling and counselling. **Wasted**.

****

Give it a stir, not too vigorous, watch that beautiful crema rise and settle.

"I'd like to stir your brains, dollop them out with this spoon!"

Only a week to go and we, the **rising** stars, were dropped, down the drain.

****

Heat the cup, not a porcelain cup, but a proper copper coffee cup.

"That should have been <u>our</u> cup, the Gala Cup, we were hot for it!"

We practically had our hands around it - it was within our **grasp**.

****

Now it's brewing, the punchy aroma in my nose is knocking

me out.

"I'd like to punch your nose, knocking you out!"

All we needed was a few more days. We could **smell** success.

****

Pour it out, gently, then the cream over the back of a spoon, just rest it on the surface.

"Your poor decision, to hold us back, was so superficial!"

We were the crème de la crème, heading straight for the **top**.

****

And now the taste, ahhh, superior and strong, nothing like proper coffee from a proper copper coffee cup.

"Your worst weakness left such a bad taste in my mouth!"

Next year there'll be no swallowing sour-faced bellyaches, and we **will** win that cup.

3☆14. JUST ONE MAN

Megan had been to Mass every morning of the holidays, returning to throw off her hated dress and don her favourite dungarees to work on her mother's farm high up in the Welsh hills. Up there she felt free, as if she had slipped the surly bonds of earth and danced with easy grace, like Maria, on the windswept heights. It was her dream, also, to become a nun and serve the whole of mankind rather than just one man. Her only doubt was that she would never be good enough.

Growing up without a father, she had always felt a hole deep in her psyche that she could never fill. Her two brothers were tall, strong and handsome but the farm took all their time and she only really saw them when she was out with them in the fields, covered in mud or grease or sheepshit and swearing like a trooper as she pushed and pulled on ropes and ears, shearing off her femininity in the process.

So she continued her prayers as she worked, asking the Lord to guide her in her wider purpose and, if she was honest with herself, asking Him also to let Tony notice her when she returned to university in September. Not that she was serious about him, Heaven forbid! He was just one man, but the kindness he had shown when leading those hikes last year had stayed with her. His calves were nicely shaped, too, as she couldn't help noticing when following immediately behind him up those steep and stony slopes. No, he wasn't for her, but she caught her breath as she imagined him speaking to her in the pub, the next time their group came down the mountain, out of the shouting wind, tired, cold and thirsty.

Another fence post hit the ground with a thud, after she levered it off the back of the Land Rover. It was too heavy for her to lift outright, but her brothers would manhandle it into place and she was an expert with the pliers and the wire-tightener. She thought this skill must have come from all those years of pulling on the strings of the bodice she had inherited from her grandmother. Thank God she had found it in the attic. A childhood of peanut butter sandwiches had taken its toll on her figure and sometimes she wondered whether it might have been simpler if she'd just smeared the jars straight onto her tummy. But this slowly-fostered sense of low-self esteem wasn't something she could just wash off now.

Back in her room, after a sudsy hot bath, she let the towel drop and looked at herself in the long mirror. No amount of prayers is going to solve this problem, she told herself. I am fat and ugly and even if I didn't become a nun, I'd never get a man. She remembered all those Saturday evenings in the post-hike pub when Tony seemed to speak to every other girl apart from her. With a deep sigh, she let her shoulders slump, crinkling the skin on her belly and making her wince. As she sat at her dressing table, two tears fell onto her leg and, through watery eyes, she saw the smooth skin of her thigh as an expanse of orange peel.

This will never do, she told herself. Self-pity is a sin. I must take whatever God wants for me with a smile and embrace it. A wicked thought penetrated her defences and flew through her mind, leaving a window open as it left. She looked at the bodice on the bed and remembered that other dress she had found up in the attic; the red one. No, I couldn't possibly! She recoiled from the image in her mind and reached for an underwear drawer that would have made Bridget Jones proud. She wasn't sure whether it was a hot or cold breeze that blew in through that open window, but whatever it was it disturbed and parted the closed curtains of her modesty and she began to think that, before she dressed in black for the rest of her life, she should give it one more go. Next term, she decided, she would make Tony notice her and speak to her in the pub.

The last week of the holidays passed like a single day as she wore herself out on the farm and spent the evenings searching every trunk in the attic and fingering through her mother's cosmetics drawer, taking minuscule amounts of foundation, lipstick, eye shadow and rouge, hoping their absence would not be noticed. By the time she was back in her digs at uni, she had built the level of confidence she needed to put her plan into action. She dressed carefully and sat in front of her small mirror for hours until she felt she was ready. All she needed now, before seeing Tony, was a guinea pig, someone who could give her the reaction she sought without actually wanting her sexually. Father David at the chaplaincy, of course, the perfect man to talk to about her desires. She took one last look at herself in the wardrobe mirror and lifted the folds of her red dress over her white stilettos and practically tripped out of the door.

The warmth of the mahogany panelling at the chaplaincy welcomed her like an old retainer. There was nobody here, so she walked through the games room to look in the kitchen. The kettle had just boiled and switched itself off as she peered round the door. Nobody in here, but, as she turned, a young man came out of the chapel. He was dressed in black robes with only the faintest hint of a dog collar showing at the neck. He had long dark curly hair, a smiling and serene face, and the softest brown eyes she'd ever seen. The eyes settled on hers, then dropped very slowly downward over her rouged cheeks, her scarlet lips and down past her bodiced cleavage, over her emphasised hips and finally rested on her painted toes.

"Buenas tardes," whispered a calm Spanish voice, "can I help you?"

Megan was startled and stuttered, "Oh my God! I mean, oh my, ah… is Father David here?"

"No, I'm afraid his sister is very ill and he has gone to look after her. My name is Father Javier and the Bishop has asked me to hold the fort until he returns."

The young priest took in Megan's distress, the alarm in her expression, and offered her a deviation. "Your word fort is from the Latin, *fortis*, meaning strong, is it not? And I've already felt that this Chaplaincy is a place of strength for students. From your eyes, too, I can see that you have strength inside. You must feel at home here?" He pronounced the word "home" with an aspirated "h".

"Ho-o-o-ome?" Megan repeated slowly, in a long drawn out breath, her eyes still wide. She was completely oblivious now, to how she looked, or to anything else in her line of sight, other than just one man, standing quietly in front of her, smiling.

3☆15. BEYOND THE PALE

We drink from silver tankards and bulbous Deutsche rummers while they bow their heads down low to sup from streams.

We eat beef and mutton and pork as they herd their cows, sheep and pigs across the bog, turf deep in blood.

We dress in Italian finery with Chinese silks while their ringless fingers clasp their fraying rags around their scrawny necks, scarred deeply by the slavish collar and the Norman noose.

We rule in comfort from our stone castle halls, warmed by fires and Viking pedigree while they shiver in their squalor in the ceaseless rain beyond the Pale.

3☆16. MARCIE

Marcie was the sweetest, darndest, nicest person I've ever known. She'd have given Hitler the benefit of the doubt. In her eyes, nobody could do any wrong other than through unfortunate accident, a mistaken slip here, an unintentional throw of the dice of life there.

As for me, I'm not so naïve. Sure I want to go to heaven, but while I'm down here on earth I'll fight the bastards off with whatever I find to hand. They don't fool me. They deserve what's coming to them.

Like that frigging freak who did for Marcie. If I ever catch up with him I'll show him sweet and nice, wrapped around a twelve-bore. Do I blame myself? Hell no, but it shouldn't have happened all the same.

It was Easter Sunday and Marcie's birthday. We were late getting to the mall for lunch and all the parking spaces were full. Well, I say all, there was just this one half-space against a wall beside some jerk who'd left his bright-red phallus at an angle across the line, taking up almost two bays. A redneck Dodge Ram 3500 4x4. I ask you, who needs one of those in a city? The mentality glowed with the paintwork and shouted from the two bumper stickers. On the driver's side: "If you can read this, stick your tongue out and lick my ass." Competing for crassness on the passenger side: "I've never had a parrot, but I've had a cockatoo."

"You won't get it in there, Marcie," I told her. But she insisted on shunting backwards and forwards until she had squeezed the tiny Nissan up against the brickwork, all the time giving this prick the benefit of her sainthood.

"Don't worry Jeb, I can get out your side. The poor chap probably couldn't see the line, it's such a big car. If it was mine, I'm sure I couldn't even get it through the entrance. So he's done quite well really, to park it at all."

Marcie understated everything. Big car? More like gas-guzzling, rhino-fucking, bullhorn-bearing, fender-bending bastard of a car. So I couldn't help myself, could I? As I opened my door, I gave it an extra nudge and left a thin blue line on his polished coachwork. That'll teach him to be such an inconsiderate bunghole. Stick your tongue out on that one!

Marcie hadn't noticed and demurely lifted her trousered legs over the console. She wouldn't have cared if she'd had a skirt on, in her world nobody would sneak a look. But I would have. Why not? Marcie was a real corker and he got it right, didn't he, that bloke who said "God make me good, but not yet."

The mall was more crowded than a Steelers-Packers game. I couldn't hear myself think and, worse, the restaurants had queues longer than the New York marathon, all pushing and shoving for their place.

"We should leave, Marcie," I said in a strained voice, "let's go find a little place out of town."

But just then a couple stood up at the edge of a burger bar, right beside us. I say "couple" but perhaps I meant "pod" because these two between them had more blubber than Seaworld. Man, they were enormous. Their bellies dropped disgustingly over jeans that could have divorced them for cruelty. Their cheap-fabric jackets Michelined out over arms that could have cofferdammed the Brooklyn Bridge. Chins tripled and quadrupled like layers on a wedding cake, each one with extra icing. As they passed us, the "male" flicked a white baseball cap onto a balding beach ball head, pointed to the table, then belched like a walrus.

Marcie, as always, saw the bright side. "Oh look, Jeb, how kind of them, this will be fine."

"Fine" was not my word for what they'd left behind; a pile of super-size detritus swimming in a lake of spilled fizz. "Oh come on, Marcie, let's go," I repeated, half in despair.

"Don't be silly, Jeb, I'm hungry."

"Well you would be, after eating practically nothing for six weeks. What do you people see in Lent anyway? Why do you torture yourselves?"

"It's not torture, it's a pleasure, and if you've seen the latest medical research, eating less helps you live longer."

Oh that it had.

When we got back to the car, the crimson penis had gone. I opened the door for Marcie and only then remembered that it was her birthday. We were going to buy her new shoes, but the mall had been too manic. Perhaps I could get her something else for now. Reluctantly I decided to re-enter the hell.

175

"Hey, Marcie, I've got to do something. You go home and I'll see you later. It won't take long."

"That's OK, Jeb, I want to call in and see mother anyway."

There she was again, turning other people's failings into opportunities for good.

What I bought was more ambitious than practical, a kind of religious perversion of the traditional nightie. "Gossamer" the assistant had said. Yeah, whatever, I was never going to see it, was I? But I allowed myself the faintest glimpse in my mind, so I wasn't really paying attention when I walked down the back steps and out by the cark park exit, until the sirens woke me up.

Marcie's Nissan was mangled against the barrier, surrounded by cops, paramedics and emergency workers. On the trunk, the clear impression of bull bars. On the concrete under the car, stained with oil and blood, a white baseball cap.

Now when I'm chewing the fat with my memories I ask myself, what was it that Marcie said in the burger bar? "It's not their fault, Jeb. They're just normal people, going about their lives."

They should put that on her headstone.

3☆17. SIZAR

So here I am, paying for my tuition with meniality, but receiving it nonetheless, a sizar at Trinity.

As I prepare victuals for the sustenance of my fellows, so my Fellows provide me with food for thought. And such unbelievable ideas come as I don my thinking cap and swim through the sea of my imagination made solid reality by experiment and wide-eyed observation.

Empirical manna falls from heaven into my lap as I lay their bread out on the plates, spooning gravy over the meat of learned men, learning as I do, an unrepentant servant of a greater good.

3☆18. THE GEOGRAPHY TEACHER

Over these last thirty years it has given me bilious attacks, ulcerative colitis, eczema and a morbid fear of travelling away from the small village in the Cotswolds that I knew as home. It was this last affliction that was the most debilitating and nonsensical for a geography teacher.

Growing up with a fascination for life around me and the world I lived in, I had studied ancient charts and maps as soon as I could read. The blue and green globes I kept in my room gave me a sense of place and a deep feeling of connection with the planet. I passed my geography degree at a college only twenty miles away and went on to a doctorate there, hoping afterwards to teach in the great universities of Europe and North America.

After my finals I was exhausted and not thinking clearly and in that hiatus between downing the examination pen and donning the academic cap, I was somehow bundled by a friend into an old woman's tent at a summer fair on the pretext of finding out whether I had passed. She ignored my question entirely and said instead that I would die somewhere far away. Just like that. I would die. Far away. Then as I was leaving she said "Goodbye Doctor."

I had sweated for six years for that title and now I found myself hoping against hope that I had failed, because then she would be wrong about the far away thing. It was stupid, I know, but it reached inside me and squeezed. It scratched at my skin and kept me awake at night, going over all those charts that I had memorised since childhood, searching for some clue as to where it might be. That place where I would die.

After sleepwalking through the graduation ceremony and falling into an SSRI stupor, I had to concede a terrible defeat. I was ill, not functioning, putting the milk in the oven and my socks in the bread bin. My father took me to one side and constructed the most convincing argument that I should seek a place at the local school as a geography master, but only, of course, until I felt well enough to apply for a post abroad. The head teacher was surprised that a star pupil should want to return. He saw it as loyalty to alma mater, a loyalty that was shown by a progressively longer and longer tenure in the post. A year, two, five, ten, twenty and then thirty years slipped down between the pages of my atlas. Ceremonies came and went; marriage, christenings, anniversaries.

At the surgery, with my visits becoming chronic, they couldn't understand. "You have a good life here," said Dr Henderson, "a respected position in our community, a loving wife, three wonderful children…." And still I didn't tell him. Then three months ago he came round to my side of the desk, put his hand on my shoulder and said, "I'm afraid it's now terminal and you should put your affairs in order."

It took twelve weeks of handholding and unfocused signing where they guided my hand to reach a point where I could, at last, go where I had wanted to go all my life. My wife stayed at home, persuaded that I had enough time to cleanse my spiritual needs and return to her. Without understanding why I had chosen this destination, I bought an air ticket to the midwest, the Great Plains where you can see miles and miles of geography in every direction.

That morning, I had driven to a dried-up river bed and sat down with the guide I had found, a storyteller from the Blackfoot tradition. He was the first person that I had ever told about my secret. He listened for an hour and then began talking very slowly. "There are three ways of understanding your secret." He took a sun-baked root out of a pouch, broke a piece off and told me to chew on it. It tasted bitter, but soothing.

"You will die in a place far away." He said in a low voice, his eyes drifting towards the horizon. "Far away is not distance, it is time and depth." I found my breath slowing and deepening.

"Before you die, you must die to the bond to this place wherever you are, which holds you but which is not you." My eyes became heavy and my vision slightly blurred.

"Then as you die, you must go to that place beyond the life you have known, to a different place far away, back to the place from which you have come." I passed out.

In a hospital in the Cotswolds, my family were around me. They were crying as I felt myself sliding off the bed, onto the ground, the dusty ground of a dried-up river bed. I felt stones around me and my head slumped forwards; it was so heavy. The sky darkened to dusk and my hearing dulled. With a last effort, I lifted my eyes and saw in front of me a shaman, cloaked in black feathers with the head of a crow.

I spread my wings.

3☆19. MEN OF GOD

Abby looked closely at the dandelion clock. She loved this moment, when the faeries were still gathered together in a white ball of wispy cotton, as if chattering softly, taking their leave of one another before the flight. Then, with a breath of laughter, she blew them off their feet, up into the air to hang gently before catching the wind and sailing away on their journey. She watched as many as she could, to see where they went, wondering whether her own soul would end up like this, as a tiny feathery parachute falling back to earth to start again. That's what her mother always told her, that she would live again and again, so many lives to enjoy.

When the real faeries came, it took the Men of God weeks even to begin to understand what was happening, and then they didn't call them faeries, they called them devils.

The first to notice that something was amiss was the Reverend Sapple. He mounted the dark wooden steps of his pulpit to begin his sermon and there, in the front pew, was his faithful verger, chuckling. A stern knitted-eyebrow stare had no effect. The verger simply responded by bursting out with loud laughter, so forceful that he fell forwards onto his knees. Fortunately, his wife ushered him out quickly enough so that the Reverend could continue his address to the rest of his flock.

The following week, his church was noticeably emptier than usual.

In the synagogue, the Rabbi Goldstein was dumbstruck when he heard shouts of "whatever" coming from the back row. This was blasphemy.

When, a fortnight later, the religious leaders came together in an emergency meeting, to compare their experiences, they all agreed that the devil was at work. By now, half of their congregations had stopped attending services and most of the others were distracted, to say the least. It was almost as if they didn't care anymore.

The news broke on a TV bulletin, sanitised for lay consumption. Storm clouds, they said, had lifted tiny seeds from an illegal opium farm over the border and carried them hundreds of miles until they floated above the city and drifted slowly down into the air we breathe, causing hallucinations. Reverend Sapple and Rabbi Goldstein were both interviewed, calling this an abomination, a plague of drug-induced hysteria.

A government spokesman announced that they were planning to drive the storm clouds out over the ocean. He didn't say how. In the meantime he advised that everybody should stay inside, close all windows and turn the central heating up. He didn't say why. In fact, he didn't say anything else at all. In bars around the city, the news was met with ribald laughter. But in church halls and meeting rooms across the metropolis, ecumenical committees had formed to co-ordinate volunteers to stoke up the brownstone and high-rise boilers to force air upwards and out through the ducts.

Back in her apartment, Abby watched her mother laying pastry in the bottom and around the sides of a pie dish. She leaned over, the better to see the thumb-prints round the edges. Only that morning, she had walked carefully along the top of the backyard wall around the clothes-lines, placing each foot in front of the other, step by step. She imagined her mother's prints as footsteps, made by invisible faeries.

"Mummy, why did I have to come inside?"

"No special reason, dear; you can sprinkle the sultanas over the apple if you like, only a few mind."

Abby sprinkled.

"Where's Daddy? "

Mummy sang a song, her voice slow and calm, stopping only to say "He's watching the game over at Ted's. He'll be back later."

Abby cupped some of the sultanas and brought her hand up to her mouth, watching her mother out of the corner of her eye, anticipating tacit approval. She chewed quietly without even a hint of guilt, then swallowed and asked,

"Mummy, why are those Men of God in the basement?"

3☆20. ON THE SURFACE

On the surface, she had every symptom of Alzheimer's.

She could never remember his name and she wittered on and on about the need to put foil on the windows, "to keep them out." But there was something in the back of Dan's mind that teased cloudy recollections out of the depths of his cellular memories and niggled his neurons.

What was it that his mother used to say to the neighbours when he was a babe in her arms? Gold leaf was best? It made no sense. He shook his head and bent down to kiss her on the forehead.

These visits were draining his appetite for life. He felt as if his energy just trickled out through his fingers and toes, oozed out through his skin, a gradual but reverse osmosis.

He told the nurse that he'd be back in a week, that he had to make a run upstate to see his father. He'd take him some winter clothes and listen to the same old stories, about how mom wasn't the same woman he'd married. He wasn't talking about now, but twenty years ago, when he had finally walked out. He lived a simple life these days, with very few human friends, but happy enough in the woods with his animals.

On the surface, pa seemed sad, but Dan always came away with a sense of renewal, a feeling that somehow his batteries had been recharged.

3☆21. CACTUS FLOWER

I know you think I'm prickly and unattractive, growing barren in my little pot, but inside I'm bursting with love.

Have patience and you'll see, for after twenty-six years I will push out a flower of such beauty that your eyes will melt and you will fall for me all over again.

3☆22. WHO TAKES THE RISK?

November 30

Inside the envelope was a ticket for the ceremony and a note, which read, "Meet me for dinner. Foyer 8pm, December 10." So she hadn't forgotten me, even after all this time. I'd followed her career through the media, but it would be good to see her again, in the flesh, and chat quietly, about how life had treated us since we last met. I doubted that we'd spend much time talking about me; I wasn't the one collecting such a prestigious prize in Economics.

December 10

She was in the foyer, as she had promised, with a latte in one hand and a newspaper on her lap. She'd seen me first and had fixed me with her eyes, but had made no move. Thirty-five years stood between now and our last meeting and I hardly knew what to do or what to say. Dumbfounded, practicalities came to the rescue, as always - such a man thing, as my wife used to say.

"Elizabeth, you're here, I mean, of course you are, but the official dinner, the banquet? How did you manage to get away? I'm sorry, what I really mean is, you look, wonderful."

Without taking her eyes off mine, she put the cup down and stood up, the paper sliding onto the floor, and took both my hands in hers. Her voice drifted into my consciousness from somewhere.

"Oh, don't worry about them, they won't miss a little old woman. Female winners, Jonathan, are still a *subheading* on their website. And the whole thing's a sham anyway, only dreamed up by a rich man to ensure he had a suitably glowing obituary, and that nobody would ever forget him. How pompous is that?"

She hadn't changed. Still the same dry sense of humour with a tinge of arsenic but, in spite of her age, no old lace as yet. She pulled me down onto the sofa and wrapped her fingers in mine. She spoke with the same soft voice that carried, at a lower timbre, more energy than you could pack in a stick of dynamite.

"Come now, you must tell all. I've been so busy for so long I haven't had time to breathe, but after today I'm going to take a year's sabbatical to catch up with old friends and live wildly before any grubby little obit hack gets his pen around my career."

So she wanted to know about me after all, this world-feted, uncompromisingly influential woman who had single-handedly turned the global economy on its head. This demi-goddess who had stepped in after the banking crisis, wrested power from a cartel of financial despots and sprayed it all over the world in tiny droplets that fell on each and every one of us. Nothing had been the same since. In my head I remembered our first discussion, held in earnest over Margherita and merlot.

"It's not about equality, Jonathan. I was the youngest of six and I never heard my parents mention the word. And they were right. It's

*about sharing, but in a responsible way. I would no more have
shared my second sister's pair of ballet shoes or my third brother's
moped than the eldest would have wanted my copy of Adam Smith's
Wealth of Nations. But we all had a say over dinner about what
money and time should be spent where and why. The good of the
family was all that mattered and we all shared in that. One day, that
family will be the world."*

At the time I had laughed it off as youthful nonsense, but
she'd done it. She'd made it happen. And here she was
talking to me again. I looked down at our hands and she
laughed.

"Jonathan, my dear boy, still haunted by doubt, aren't you?
Well you shouldn't be. You know it was you, don't you, who
inspired me to do what I did. You're the reason I'm here
today, for the Prize, and you're the reason why I'm here
tonight."

"Me?"

"Yes, you. Do you remember that evening, when we had that
dinner, and you talked about work all night?"

How could I forget it? The highest and lowest points in my
life separated by a pizza and a glass of wine. I looked back at
her eyes. They urged me to tell the story again.

"You're talking about the old buffoon, aren't you? In that
dinosaur insurance company where we were writing the IT
strategy? Ha ha! Oh yes! I remember. You were on my team
then, imagine that, you working for me. It beggars belief. But
we had a difficult job to do and I'd ask for the best. So you,
with your freshly-inked PhD, wanting to test your theories

and prove your worth, came to twist us all around your little finger. We were top-rated, our team, hand-picked, the very best, and he knew it, the silly old bugger, sitting in his mahogany-walled office with his single malt in the cabinet. He and his ilk, all far too comfortable, so I poked his pride and asked him for the keys to the executive washrooms, for my team. He must have been forewarned, because he opened a drawer and put a key down on the desk in front of me."

Her eyes opened wider, prompting me to go on.

"That's one key, I said to him, but what about the other? The sly old fox pretended he didn't know what I was talking about. At least I thought he was pretending. If that's the key to the men's, I said, where's the key to the women's? The women's what? he asked. *The women's executive washroom, of course.* He was staring at me, blankly, his mouth opening slowly. If he was pretending, then he was a bloody good actor. But the truth hit me that he was serious. He wasn't a sly old fox at all, just a silly old goat. He sat up straight and put his fists on the desk, his stare turning to glare, and said half laughing and half incredulous: "What are you talking about? Why would we have a women's executive washroom? *We don't have women executives!!!*"

My own voice was becoming strained and she put a finger over my lips to stop me talking.

"That's what I remember you telling me," she said. "That was the moment when everything fell into place, when I knew how to make it all happen."

"What? How?"

"It was simple really. That executive, and his fear, taught me more about hierarchy than any textbook I'd ever read. He was blustery, yes, but he was only protecting what was his, as he saw it. And that was the lightbulb moment, *how he saw the world*."

"Lightbulb moment?"

"Yes. Financial corporations, and by that I mean the banks, were keen to embrace the new technology that we brought to them. They were gagging for it, but there was an important difference between them and the insurance companies, and an even more important difference between their cultures."

"I'm not following you."

"Think of it this way. Banks drive the economy, because they are the hunters, the hungry innovators. They invest their money all over the world. Very adventurous, and very masculine. But in earlier days insurance companies held the real power, because they were the long stop. Without them, nobody took any real risks. Remember how Lloyds came into being in a smoky coffee shop, because merchants needed to insure their ships? So while their vessels and investments sailed the seas, facing shipwreck and piracy and all kinds of dangers, their insurance premiums stayed safely in London. The underwriters built up large funds and sat on them, ready to compensate merchants and widows. More motherly than manly, don't you think?"

"What are you getting at?" I scrunched my eyebrows, suggesting confusion.

"When we worked together, back in the 80s, banking was just

beginning to change, with women cracking the glass ceilings, but they did so because they were women who thought like men. When we were chatting over dinner that night, I understood your macho approach to the challenge you had faced, and it contrasted sharply with that executive's very different, defensive response. As you were talking, it struck me that insurance companies were run by men who thought like women, even though they'd never admit it."

My mouth opened, but I couldn't think of anything to say, so I just stared at her and listened.

"Banking is about individual risk and profit for the few, but insurance works on the law of large numbers and sufficiency for all, and it needs a different way of thinking to manage it. Inclusivity is much more of a feminine philosophy. So that was the way forwards, adopt an insurance approach, spread the risks, and the rewards, to meet the needs of the many, and to do that we had to change the culture."

I raised my eyebrows and ventured a guess.

"You mean, taking a kind of feminine, protective, sharing attitude to managing risk, instead of a masculine, adventurous, winner-takes-all one?"

"Exactly, it's all about who takes the risk, and who shares in the rewards, and what those rewards are, and how they are seen. Unfortunately, just as we were making headway, there was another sea-change. Banks were adapting our new technology to push boundaries, to explore and grow, but insurers began using it to control their exposure, to become more selective, and to shrink their risk. So then, when you tried to buy a policy, unless you fitted their database profiles, you were excluded."

"Computer says no?"

"Yes. Well, almost. *Insurance* computer says no, but *banking* computer says yes. So we had an ever-widening gap between financial flows and the risks they need to cover. The 2008 crash was just a symptom, it wasn't the disease, nor was it the cure. Austerity, poverty, inequality, they were all inevitable results of algorithms."

"How could you do anything about those?"

"Look around us, all these smartphones, the world is connected now. When people wake up, they're powerful. They vote, with poll cards, and their feet, *and their clicks*. If you're fast enough, you can anticipate shifts and catch the attention of the social media giants, and then they will listen."

"I'm guessing that's what you did. What did you say to them?"

"We asked them to change the algorithms. We asked them to adapt the underlying assumptions on which calculations are made. We mapped trends and argued that they would only retain relevance if they moved their focus from growth to sufficiency, from profit to provision, from speed to stamina. All very simple really, but oh so powerful. Think of it like irrigation. Instead a few pipes pouring all the world's water into fewer and fewer buckets, we asked them to channel the water to sprinklers, over larger and larger areas. And they did, because they understood, and it suited them."

I still couldn't get my head round all this and hid my

discomfort by continuing with the original story.

"But I made him do it, that old buffoon. He allocated another washroom just for you. That evening, you remember, I gave you the key."

She smiled and her eyes half-closed and moistened, the same eyes she'd shown me that evening so long ago.

"None of this matters any more," she whispered.

Back then, my eyes had seen her beauty and had ached. Back then, my ears had heard her words, found them confusing and believed it was hopeless. But now I heard her words and I looked into her eyes again and my heart missed a beat, because she was there, in front of me, calling, returning the ache.

In that instant I realised that, thirty-five years before, in thinking I was being dashing and virile and clever, by solving a gender issue with a symbolic key, I had completely missed the point.

AFTERWORD

Thank you for reading these stories.

If you liked them, please leave a review on Amazon. This should not take you long, but it may help others to decide whether they might like to read them too.

Thank you again.

NOTES

Vol.1 ☆

1☆1. Poseidon Prompts

This is about exploring the possibility of colonizing other planets. The central theme is the need for water, an issue that is becoming increasingly important even here on Earth.

The cast are members of the Outlander Team, which is leading the move into space, so they are testing a new technique to stimulate thinking, hoping that this might lead to some creative solutions. The prompts used in the narrative are the same as those which suggested the story.

The original title was Tyro, a word meaning novice or someone who is just beginning to learn a skill. Also, in Greek mythology, Tyro was the mother of Poseidon's twin sons.

1☆2. Shortening the Odds

He was taking his holiday in the third week in July, the same week that the four co-eds had booked their cabin. He had blocked all other bookings and was going to be the only man at the resort. This was his idea of fighting his battles on his own ground.

1☆3. The Green Man

Paige had killed Ed and bricked him up in the recess between the fireplace and the outside wall. She plastered the wall and added the face of a Green Man, from English folklore.

Using plaster to mould decoration on walls is called pargetting, which is why I called her Paige Etting. As a born writer, her maiden name was Paige Turner. Her husband was Ed Etting (editing) her work.

1☆4. Cutting a Dash and Pasting It

I used a powerful program called Scrivener to write, edit, format and compile this book, but before technology changed the world of publishing, editors would literally *cut* out pictures and letters *and paste* them onto a layout. When the new software generation arrived, some publications resisted and held on to the old way of doing things. This story harks back to those days.

1☆5. Privy Councillor

When Dylan was a child, his father used to lock him in the outside loo, aka the privy, as a punishment. He never forgot the experience and, as an adult, he became a councillor and founded the Orchard Project to support youngsters in trouble with the law and keep them out of jail.

Now that his father is dying and his sister wants him to help in the final months, he cannot forgive. He refuses to visit his father, deciding that the project is more important.

1☆6. Plantation

I have known men who lived for love in this way. They spent decades "building" careers and homes for their women, only to leave it all behind, preferring to live more simply when the relationship came to an end.

I have also known both men and women who have that far away look in their eyes. It can be slightly disconcerting if you don't know whether you are truly connecting with someone.

There is more sadness behind this story than I was able to portray at the time.

1☆7. Sun, Sea, Susan

From my own experience, I know that Speech Therapy can be very effective. It is a wide and fascinating field with many interesting techniques. That is not to say that all of them are necessarily conventional.

1☆8. Mother Dear Father

Since this story was written, awareness of gender dysphoria has increased significantly, particularly amongst our younger population.

Gender reassignment surgery is becoming more common and more acceptable.

1☆9. Children's Corner

Children's Corner is a musical suite by Claude Debussy,

written for his three-year old daughter, Chouchou.

He dedicated the suite with the words:

"A ma chère petite Chouchou, avec les tendres excuses de son Père pour ce qui va suivre."

(To my dear little Chouchou, with tender apologies from her father for what follows.)

I have borrowed the second phrase to make my own excuses for this scenario based on what might have happened after the end bang of the first piece. The subjects in the suite, the elephant, porcelain doll, snow, shepherd's flock, Golliwogg, and the cake prize all play a part in this story.

The Golliwogg was a fictional character in children's books by Florence Upton, popular in the first decade of the twentieth century when the suite was written and after which Debussy named his cakewalk.

1☆10. Premonition

We all have times when we think we know something, but cannot quite put our finger on what it is. These premonitions can last for years before an event turns the feeling into a reality, sometimes happily, but sometimes with unexpected tragedy.

1☆11. Such Small Hands

On a simple level, this is a love story about a relationship. On a deeper level, in psychotherapy there is a theory about "Part Object Relations" which looks at how, at a very early age, we learn to relate to others emotionally through their parts, e.g. hands, rather than with the whole person.

Academic papers have been written about this subject, but I prefer it as a simple love story.

1☆12. Remedial Consequences

Do you know a Sally? Someone who believes in alternative medicine, using plants and herbs? Most practitioners are highly skilled and enormously helpful, but dabblers, who are not always competent, can be dangerous.

Personally, I never pick mushrooms in the wild as I just don't trust myself not to make a mistake. But what is seriously scary about Sally is that she is prepared to cover up her mistakes at any cost.

1☆13. Lust in Translation

OK, hands up, I was having a little fun. Juvenile humour really, remembered from my first encounter with *Obst mit Schlag*, way back when, but harmless I hope.

1☆14. Herorist

Reading this again in 2018, I find it chilling. It is historical in tone, but could it happen in the 21st century? Back then there were only the basic revolutionary tools of printing press and soapbox, but today we have the internet and social media. So I have to remind myself that it is fiction.

It is fiction!

Isn't it?

1☆15. Iron Age Forty-Fiscations

We tend to think of red tape as a modern phenomenon, but rules of administration date from the dawn of history.

When Alfred the Great introduced his "Doom Book" in 892 A.D. he was collating earlier codes. (Doom here means law, and is unrelated to William I's Doomsday Book, which was an audit of the kingdom nearly 200 years later.)

Of course, as soon as you had rules, along came bribery to bend them (in the name of keeping the peace, of course).

1☆16. Capo

The main character here is a combination of a talented young musician I know who never goes anywhere without his capo, and Colin, the irrepressible optimist in *Love Actually*, who went to America believing he would be appreciated there.

1☆17. Unsettled

There is a time loop here that isn't meant to meet at each end; rather it overlaps, like a spiral.

The story hints at a Shiva, or Job-like destruction of the comfort of an overly sophisticated life that is too detached from the natural world.

It is not clear whether the force that destroys his life is external or internal; that question is left hanging.

1☆18. Gravesend Quarry

Whilst there were quarries at Gravesend (in Kent, UK) which have been turned into housing, this story title has another more gruesome meaning.

Terry was distraught at losing his rabbit's foot, which he decided had been buried in the teenage biker's grave. When he heard that the grave was going to be moved, his quarry (what he was hunting) would be found in the grave's end location.

Greaser was a slang term for biker, on both sides of the Atlantic.

1☆19. But Not Yet!

The old story goes that St Augustine was a bit of a lad who fully enjoyed the sins of the flesh before he became more pious.

His most quoted prayer is "Please God, make me good, *but not yet!*"

1☆20. Granmardi Gras

Three generations of women are celebrated here, through Estelle, Rosalind, and Millie.

The struggle for women's rights are reflected in their life stories and, correspondingly, in their personalities and attitudes.

The purple, green and white of Estelle's Two Piece were the

colours of the suffragette movement.

Now the three generations are going to take part in the famous Mardi Gras festival together, on the 100th anniversary of International Women's Day.

1☆21. Prompted Blindness

When we hear the name, Sir Isaac Newton, we think of his laws of physics. Very dry. But the personal circumstances of his life were complicated, full of strong emotions, often bordering on jaw-dropping.

1☆22. Aurora

This story draws inspiration from the 1989 film "When Harry met Sally" and the 1970 French film "Claire's Knee". There is also an indirect reference to *The Dice Man*, a 1971 controversial novel by Luke Rhinehart.

The main character here has a lifelong irritation with social expectations that his friendships should fit into a sexual framework, hindering them from evolving in other dimensions. He believes that gender stereotypes should not constrain how any of us interact with our fellow humans.

Vol.2☆☆☆☆☆☆☆☆☆☆☆☆☆☆☆☆☆☆☆☆☆☆☆☆☆☆☆☆☆☆☆☆

2☆1. The Pedant's Wife

One of the reasons I love writing flash fiction to prompts is that I never know what I'm going to see until I press the button, and I never quite know what I'm going to write until

I've written it. Sometimes a story will evolve of its own accord as my fingers are hitting the keys. It is as if hands and eyes are operating independently, creating and observing as two different people. This is one such story.

2☆2. "Hello World"

I could explain what *int data types* and *compound assignment operators* are here, but that would be to miss the point.

We live increasingly in a world designed and programmed by "Geeks" and even if they explained what they were doing, we wouldn't necessarily understand a word of it.

It's not just about the money any more, it's about what and who influences the thinking that provides the votes that justify the power.

"Hello World!"

2☆3. The Freedom

The time frame mentioned by Cal White is STE - Solanum Tuberosum Era (potato era) - and dates from 8000 BC when potatoes were first cultivated.

The story is ecological at heart, with a positive message that it is still possible to save the planet, following a change in values, even if it will take a long time.

Potato varieties used as names here include: CalWhite, Kanona, Katahdin, Kennebec, Krantz, Russet Norking, Red La Soda, Norland, Shepody, Norwis, Pike, Sebago, Monona.

2☆4. PGAD

This woman is being interviewed by a journalist and what she is talking about is no joke.

The International Society for Sexual Medicine (ISSM) describes PGAD as "persistent, unwanted and distressing." It was not identified until 2001 and, although extreme cases have led to suicides, PGAD is still "not recognized as a clinical disorder in the DSM-IV-TR or the International Classification of Diseases (ICD-10)."

You can read more on the ISSM website at:
   professionals.issm.info/news/research-summaries/female-sexual-arousal-disorders/

and there is a very informative article in the Guardian newspaper at:
   www.theguardian.com/lifeandstyle/2014/apr/14/women-persistent-genital-arousal-disorder-orgasm-pgad-pain

2☆5. Treebound

This was a story that wrote itself. It just unfolded. So I am not completely sure how to explain it. I can feel the tree, its weight and its gravity, but the narrator is harder to grasp. I think perhaps he might be a young man who died after riding his motorcycle into the tree.

2☆6. Monetary Crisis

Written in 2011, this story imagines what might have happened if the UK had joined the Eurozone as the European

Debt Crisis was growing and confidence in banking systems was plummeting - a very worrying time.

Unsurprisingly, the burden is passed all the way down from the top to the ordinary people in their everyday lives.

N.Euro (Northern Euro) here is the name given to the new currency in the UK. Unofficial credit is sometimes called buying "on tick", so someone controlling this in N.Euros, at this very worrying time, is a *neurotic* policeman.

2☆7. Chemistry Set

In one of those insane moments that writers have now and again, I began pondering the transience of the thirty trillion cells in the human body. Then one of the website prompts reminded me and this story came out.

2☆8. Matricide

Going back to those thirty trillion cells in the body, mentioned in Chemistry Set, their levels of communication and organisation put our warring seven billion human beings to shame.

Every cell has the DNA blueprint for the whole body, not just its own function. So, as we are beginning to discover, any cell can become any other cell. Communication between cells, to adopt a particular role (e.g. in an organ), suggests a form of agreement between them (contract, if you will), which we do not yet fully understand.

Meiosis (one from two) is the reproductive method we call sex. Mitosis (two from one) is the method we call cloning (as in Dolly the sheep).

Why did our species evolve to favour meiosis?

How did meiosis come to favour the male sex? What implications does this method of reproduction have for our social structures, and our resulting ability to communicate and organise as human beings?

2☆9. The Ideal Homo Sapiens Exhibition

Whilst Matricide took a serious, if pseudo-scientific, view of gender discrimination, this story pokes a little fun at the topic, from a feminine perspective.

The scene is set in 1908. Frances (Fanny, a popular name in those days) is a well-to-do thrill-seeking lady about town in the reign of Edward VII.

In that year, the summer Olympics, held at White City, London, lasted for over six months. The Franco-British Exhibition was held alongside and featured "colonial villages" which would fail every test of taste and political correctness today. In July 1908 the Allied Artists Association held their first exhibition to promote Modernism. The month before, the Suffragette movement held their first major rally in London, and it became fashionable to display their colours of purple, white and green.

This story, of course, has no connection with The Ideal Home Exhibition, first held at Olympia in London in 1908.

NB : Pulchritude is from the Latin pulchritudo, meaning physical beauty and excellence.

2☆10. Anders Celsius

I am sure Uppsala is nothing like the wilderness portrayed here, looking back, as the story does, some 300 years.

The theme is based on an old article in my Institute of Management magazine which, from memory, suggested that our careers "bumble along" unfolding as events take them, rather than by following any particular plan.

Celsius had a brilliant brain and quite possibly could have done anything, but he did what he did because, well, perhaps that's just how events unfolded.

2☆11. Writer's Block

This happened. One day I logged onto the website, clicked on the prompts, and couldn't make head nor tail of them. So I boiled the kettle and took a cup of tea out into the garden, to sit and ponder and look at the flowers. With only 20 minutes or so to go, I used the prompts to write this stream of consciousness.

2☆12. Word Massage

At some point in the dim and distant past, to gain a better understanding of stress in the workplace, I studied for a diploma in Anatomy, Physiology & Swedish Massage.

One of the enduring memories of that time was the release of deep body rhythms, the patterns, the flow, the tempo and cadences.

2☆13. The Suppuration of Independant Seperation

When online dating was becoming popular, I asked some participants what their biggest bugbears with it were.

The men highlighted specifics like poor spelling and use of hackneyed phrases e.g. "happy in your own skin."

The women were more generic and just pointed to what they saw as a high incidence of unbelievable arrogance.

2☆14. For Theo, Rex and Patricia

In case you've missed it, these three names are derived from the Latin for God, King and Country. In the west the elite are brought up with these values and, if they follow the rules and remain within the establishment then, by and large, they will be looked after. Retirement is no problem and they may even get a gong.

NB - use of the year 1908 here is pure coincidence and is not connected to the story about the Ideal Homo Sapiens Exhibition, above.

2☆15. Day of the Jackal

Gestalt can be serious; but it doesn't have to be. You can have fun, as long as it helps to understand what is really going on.

Fritz Perls, who developed the therapy, described three levels of talking that avoid the issues:
    a) chicken-shit - irrelevant chit chat
    b) bull-shit - quite simply, lies

c) elephant-shit - grandiose philosophy.

If you can find a way of communicating that cuts through all the layers of shit, then you're on to a winner.

2☆16. Lines in the Sand

Over the years since my youth I have written in all formats. Other than for my poetry, which has a will of its own, my mind has always insisted on having the title "Editor" inscribed in gold on a polished wooden panel on its desk. But when writing this very short piece, my first ever flash, with a 90 minute time limit, I reached peak frustration after an hour, then picked up that titular panel and threw it out of the window.

So this story was written in 30 minutes whilst my editor mind was outside the building, retrieving the all-important symbol of power and control.

Back in the office, with big red pen poised behind the replaced panel, my mind had no idea how to edit it because, amongst the confusion and absurdities, the words make a kind of sense and, deep down, I think I know where to find those lines in the sand.

2☆17. Extra Sibling Protection

Do you have a brother or sister? Do you sometimes know what they're thinking? Can you imagine knowing everything they are doing? Wherever they are? All the time?

Have you read *The Men Who Stare At Goats*, a non-fiction book about using paranormal skills for military purposes?

2☆18. Sacred Heart

Priests are human. This story poses the question whether they should have to choose between living a normal life or serving their God.

2☆19. The Marlowe Love Kit

Although we were brought up on Shakespeare, it was Kit Marlowe who broke the mould of Elizabethan language with his introduction of blank verse.

There is also here a nod to Nadsat, the Russian-based language invented by Anthony Burgess in *A Clockwork Orange*. This story follows predictions that future languages will be simpler and evolve out of social groupings.

2☆20. Fairy Tale

This story is based on a conversation I overheard, between two young children.

It's not supposed to make sense, but it kinda does.

2☆21. Nerida's Youth

This is a work of fiction. Names, characters, places and incidents are the product of the authors' imaginations or are used fictitiously. Any resemblance to actual events, locales, or persons, living or dead, is entirely coincidental.

That said, there are some artists whose lives and works I find utterly inspiring.

2☆22. Rain Man

Adam has a gift that was recognised and nurtured by the Native American community he lived in as a child. That tribe named him Rain Man, after the way that his gift manifested.

Later in his life, when working in corporate organisations, the same gift brought in business, as if by magic. So he was named Rain Maker. That way, his colleagues could work alongside him without having to understand him.

But once he came to the attention of psychiatrists, through a freak accident, he was diagnosed with a form of Aspergers and studied in an institution.

When his corporate associates heard about this, they called him Rain Man, only this time it was after the film, not because of his natural gift. They adapted their understanding of him: he was no longer gifted, he was mentally ill.

Vol.3☆☆☆☆☆☆☆☆☆☆☆☆☆☆☆☆☆☆☆☆☆☆☆☆☆☆☆☆☆☆☆☆

3☆1. Pharmaverbum Medisemantics

Such is the power of language. This story is meant to be amusing, but there is much truth in it. Words can be healing, if used with imagination and belief.

It is similar in a way to the "headache stones" - small round rocks about the size of oranges which we kept on the wall in the porch. By the time my youngest was five, he already knew that he could cure a headache by holding one to his temple.

At that age, almost everything is magic, and why not?

3☆2. Our Lady of Assumptions

Two powerful forces which are never far away from life are fear and the need for comfort, both of which are influenced by how we see the world.

Rose-tinted glasses is a phrase that comes to mind, but there are other colours. Quite often, they are not our glasses, but prescriptions developed for us by others, e.g., educational institutions.

When I was teaching in a university, some of my students found it helpful to talk about living in bubbles, as a prelude to bursting them, when they wanted to see the world in a different way.

3☆3. Talk and Cheese

The title suggests that these two are polar opposites, but that doesn't rule out an attraction.

Colin is struggling, but he's persevering and he may be getting somewhere.

Sabrina is amused, and being rather mischievous, but she's staying for another cola.

3☆4. Head Hunter

Ninety-five percent of this is based on truth. Fortunately the last part is not.

The head hunter I met, over thirty years ago, was a gentleman of the old school, rarely seen in the modern world of recruitment. Not for him the arm's length internet, he had the personal focused attention of a fly-fisherman up to his waist in a salmon river, with a self-assured air of confidence that he would reel in his catch, however long it took.

Such was his Edwardian-like manner that it was a natural progression to put him in this setting and add that last five percent.

3☆5. A Compulsory Experience in Solitude

This is the world we live in today, embracing and justifying to ourselves the great diaspora of progress.

3☆6. A Close Shave

Spoiler alert: Jeremiah is Sweeney Todd's grandson, and he is about to resume the family trade. It looks as if Isaiah Thornhill is about to become his first customer.

3☆7. Eliot Recollects

T. S. Eliot was for many of my generation the greatest poet. His life was not straightforward and there were many physical, emotional, geographical and personal influences.

The Frenchman referred to is Jules Laforgue, an early adopter in French of free verse and a major inspiration for Eliot. The references here to factories, skirt and eyes, and the last line are from Laforgue's poem "October's Little Miseries."

Eliot has said that the title of his poem "The Love Song of Alfred J Prufrock" might have been influenced by Kipling's poem "The Love Song of Har Dyal."

All this said, my story is a work of fiction and any interpretations I might appear to make are from my imagination.

3☆8. Tongue-tied

Every so often a new case is splashed across the tabloids and the public is horrified. How could he/she be so inhuman? Films are made, which exploit our innate feelings. Gossip goes round the dinner tables, defending whichever side we have taken.

In a private world, there is never any relief from the pain caused by family separation, supported by an adversarial legal system, which uses the language of winning and losing without ever understanding the meaning and reality of loss.

3☆9. The Task of the Day

This story was influenced by the suggestion, usually attributed to Eleanor Roosevelt, that we should do one thing everyday which scares us, raising our heart rate.

3☆10. Make Your Bed

I am not going to explain this one beyond the obvious. Four people were shipwrecked on an island. Fifteen years later, they were found by another ship. There were then fourteen of them but they decided they did not want to be rescued.

3☆11. Gooseberry Bush

This is sourced from a number of gardening websites. But then those of you who cultivate gooseberries will know that.

3☆12. Fanny Hurd

The prompt that inspired this story was the first stanza of a poem by Thomas Hardy - *Voices from Things Growing in a Churchyard*, which is:

These flowers are I, poor Fanny Hurd,
Sir or Madam,
A little girl here sepultured.
Once I flit-fluttered like a bird
Above the grass, as now I wave
In daisy shapes above my grave,
All day cheerily,
All night eerily!

3☆13. A Proper Cup

This oral triptych listens to a young swimming coach letting off steam whilst making coffee.

He is angry and frustrated because the School Principal disbanded the team after complaints from parents that their children were coming home late and exhausted every day.

I have called it an oral triptych because I wanted to capture the amazing ability to maintain a detailed focus on the process of making a great cup of coffee, and at the same time ranting wildly, whilst also following a logical path of reasoning. These are rare skills I have seen demonstrated only by the very best baristas.

3☆14. Just One Man

Although this is a simple story on the face of it, I wanted to acknowledge the pressures that we put on our children as they grow into adults.

The expectations, assumptions and put-downs can be overwhelming.

Hopefully there is a deeper primeval knowledge that can help us all make the right decisions when we are faced with them, even if those same expectations and assumptions say we cannot.

3☆15. Beyond the Pale

Here the word Pale is from the same root as palisade or, more simply, fence. It refers to the area around Dublin which was controlled directly by the King of England. It shows the gulf between the Anglo-Norman-French aristocracy and the peasantry over which they ruled.

Whilst this story harks back to the Norman invasion of Ireland beginning in in 1169, it reflects a much wider and longer history, encompassing reference to the walls of ancient cities (Jericho, Troy etc), civilisations (China, Rome) and now nation states around the world as they build yet new barriers.

Inside our walls we speak our own language and protect our customs.

Outside our walls, the "barbarians" speak in different tongues and their behaviour is seen as uncivilised and unacceptable, i.e., beyond the pale.

NB - after the Norman Conquest, the French-speaking lords had local serfs to look after the cows, sheep and pigs. So in the fields, where the work was being done, these animals had Anglo/Saxon names, but when their meat had been cooked and put on the table to eat, they became the French boeuf (beef), mouton (mutton), and porc (pork).

3☆16. Marcie

Have you been lucky enough to know a Marcie? Someone who sees the good in everyone, no matter what they do?

3☆17. Sizar

A sizar is a student who finances his/her university degree by undertaking menial tasks for fellow students, e.g., fetching meals (otherwise known as sizes).

Isaac Newton was a sizar at Trinity College, Cambridge.

3☆18. The Geography Teacher

Westerners think of geography in topographical terms, maps and areas and distances. We do not easily allow for other dimensions.

When this young PhD student heard the seer's prediction, he interpreted "far away" as distance so he stayed close to home all his life, until he had traveled in other ways, in time and depth, to arrive close to his death. Only then did he seek an alternative meaning from a different philosophy.

SSRI = Selective Seratonin Reuptake Inhibitor, a form of antidepressant.

3☆19. Men of God

Sometimes, perhaps, our crazy world is better understood if we view it through the eyes of children. You can decide for yourself what was causing the irreverent humour.

3☆20. On the Surface

Whilst it is mentioned, this story is not about Alzheimer's. As to what the real subject is, that question is left open.

Dan remembers that his mother had exhibited strange behaviour since he was a child, a behaviour that drained him of energy.

His father, who had left the home because of this behaviour, lived a very different life, one that gave energy back to Dan.

3☆21. Cactus Flower

This is very short, only 52 words, but I have included it because, for those of us who have more than 52 years behind us, it rings true.

There are many species which have a long flowering cycle. In 2013, in Wales, a Dracaena draco flowered after 25 years.

There are also some prickly people who can take a lot longer than 26 years to open up and show their flowers.

3☆22. Who Takes the Risk?

The story about the executive washroom keys is based on a real event in the 1980s. It was so outrageous that I have never forgotten it.

There was a PhD on the team, who was outstanding in her field, but I have drawn inspiration for this fictional story from present day thinking in Economic theory, together with recent developments in big data technology. There are hopeful signs in this direction.

More importantly, now that #metoo and other movements are lifting lids, we can progress our understanding of the effect of gender beliefs and behaviours on the socio-economic structures of our world.